BED

OF BONES

USA Today Bestselling Author

CHERYL

BRADSHAW

This book is a work of fiction. Names, characters, places, businesses, and incidents either are the products of the author's imagination or are used in a fictitious manner. Any similarity to events or locales or persons, living or dead, is entirely coincidental.

First edition September 2013
Copyright © 2013 by Cheryl Bradshaw
Cover Design Copyright 2013 © Reese Dante
All rights reserved.
ISBN: 1492397261
ISBN-13: 978-1492397267

DEDICATION

To Park City, Utah.
I must away.
Farewell.

ACKNOWLEDGEMENTS

There were days I wondered if I'd ever see this book through to the end, but here I sit, satisfied and ready to begin again. To my husband, thank you for appreciating my passion. Living with a writer has its challenges. For all the times I'm lost inside myself contemplating the next chapter of my book, I really am listening to you! To great friends. Thank you for loving me unconditionally and lending your ear. To my family for reading what I write. I appreciate you all. Tiffany Stewart, thank you for taking me on. You're my person. Let's do this! Janet Green (thewordverve) the best editor around, there isn't enough ways to thank you for all you've done and continue to do to make me better, my friend. To my proofers, Becky Fagnant and Amy Jirsa-Smith, I appreciate you both. Reese Dante, your covers continue to amaze. Bob Houston and Dafeenah Jameel, for excellence in formatting and for making everything beautiful. D.P. Lyle, M.D., for your forensic advice and expertise. And finally, "Saturday Smile" by Gin Wigmore is the theme song of this novel. It takes a lot of hands to steer this ship. I am truly blessed.

"At what point then is the approach of danger to be expected?

I answer, if it ever reach us, it must spring up amongst us."

–Abraham Lincoln

CHAPTER 1

JUNE 1956

PARK CITY, UTAH

Willie wiped his dirt-stained hands across the sides of his jeans and cocked his head to the side, eyeballing his younger brother, who lagged behind. "Come on, Leonard! Why ya gotta be such a drag all the time? We'll never get where we're goin' if we don't hustle."

"You're walkin' too fast," Leonard sniffed. "Wait up!"

Willie didn't turn around. He didn't stop. He didn't even slow down. He lengthened his stride and kept on going. "Quit whining, ya big baby, or next time I'll leave ya home."

Leonard kicked a pebble with his shoe. It sailed across the open field, narrowly missing Willie's head when it whizzed by. "Don't call me that!"

"What—a baby?"

"Yeah. Don't. I'm seven. Babies are…well…babies."

"Well, that's what ya are, aren't ya?" When Leonard failed to respond, Willie glanced back, knowing exactly what he'd see when he did. Leonard's face had turned as red as their dad's BMW 507—not because he was embarrassed and not because of the heat. He was about to get angry. When that happened, Leonard's forehead broke out in an overabundance of dots that made him look like he had the chicken pox. "Hey, I was just kiddin' around, Leonard. Ya know that, right?"

"Mom said we weren't allowed to go past the fence, and I can't see it anymore. We're gonna get in trouble, Willie. I just know it."

"Nothing is goin' to happen, all right? Mom and Dad won't find out unless one of us tells 'em. This is our little secret. Okay?" Willie shoved a hand inside his pocket, removed a plastic comb, and slicked it through his sandy-brown hair. At thirteen years old, he was practically a man. At least he liked to think so. He'd matured a good deal faster than all of his friends. While their voices remained high-pitched and squeaky, his was deep, like his dad's. He didn't look much like him though; he looked like his idol, James Dean. A year before when James was killed in a fatal car accident, Willie paid tribute by ditching his Chinos and collared shirts for jeans and plain white tees. He'd even talked his mother into buying him a leather jacket at Christmas to complete the look. At school he was ridiculed by his male classmates. He didn't care. None of *them* had a fifteen-year-old girlfriend. He did.

"How much longer?" Leonard mumbled. "I wanna go home."

"We will, just as soon as I find what I'm lookin' for."

"Not *this* home," Leonard said, "our *real* one. I hate it here."

Willie hated it too. Park City was the most boring place he'd ever visited in his life. Day after day they sat around with nothing to do, waiting for their dad to sign the paperwork over to a developer who had big plans for his grandfather's land. They were only supposed to be here for a week. It had been more than two. He didn't know why his dad kept going back and forth, negotiating every last detail with the realtor, and he didn't care either. All he wanted was to get back to Chicago, to his own room, his friends, and most of all, blue-eyed, blond-haired Betty.

"It's hot." Leonard wiped the sweat from his brow and flicked it into the air.

"We're almost there. Ya see it?"

"See what?"

"The hole."

"What hole?"

Willie stopped. When Leonard caught up, Willie placed his hands on his brother's head, directing him to a large, black, squarish spot on the ground several feet below.

"What is it?" Leonard asked.

"A mine shaft."

"A what?"

"Men used to go down that hole, get stuff out of the ground, and sell it. Made lots of money too, from what Dad said." Willie tested the soft dirt in front of him and then stepped forward, making his way to the bottom of the hill. "Ya best step where I step, okay? I don't need ya breakin' a leg out here. You dig?"

Leonard nodded.

"This place wasn't always a ghost town," Willie said.

Leonard swallowed—hard. "There are...ghosts here?"

Willie reached back, patting Leonard's arm. "Not real ones, dipstick. A ghost town is a place people leave behind—the buildings are still here, but not the people. Not many of them, anyway."

"Is that why most of the stores in town are closed?" Leonard asked.

"Now yer gettin' it."

"Why'd they all leave?"

"Hated it, probably. Same as us."

"Why would they leave all that money?" Leonard asked.

"Maybe it ran out. Maybe they got everything they could out of the ground and there wasn't any more left."

"Is that why grandpa moved here—for money?"

Willie shrugged. "When gramps was alive, he was in charge of a whole crew of guys. Made loads of cash and bought land with it. That's why we're here." Willie reached the opening of the mine and knelt down. "Outta sight! Leonard, check this out."

"Is it safe? It doesn't look safe."

"'Course it is. It's not like we're going in. We're just takin' a peek. Nothin' wrong with that."

Leonard bent down next to Willie. "How far down do you think it goes?"

"I dunno. Why don't ya hop on in and find out?"

Willie walked over to a rock a few feet away and pulled a pack of cigarettes out of his back pocket. He flipped one into his mouth, lit up, and took a nice, long drag.

Leonard sat on the rock next to him. "Dad know you have those?"

Willie twisted the sleeve on Leonard's shirt and yanked him close. "No, and you're not gonna tell him either."

"I won't—let go!"

The two sat in silence for the next two minutes, Willie taking occasional puffs on the cigarette and

Leonard flipping a Slinky back and forth between his hands.

Willie finished the cigarette, stood, and flicked the butt out of his hands, smashing it into the scorching earth with his foot until he couldn't see it any longer. "Come on. We'd better get back."

Leonard hopped off the rock. The Slinky slipped out of his hand and tumbled into the mouth of the shaft, catching on a patch of sagebrush just inside. "My Slinky!"

"Leave it," Willie said. "You can get another one."

"I don't want another one. I bought it with my own money. It took a whole month to save up for it." Before Willie could interject a second time, Leonard had bolted forward until he was close enough to the Slinky to reach down and grab it.

"Leonard, no!" Willie yelled. "Don't!"

The next few seconds moved like a Ferris wheel in slow motion. Leonard reached for the Slinky, but it broke free of the sagebrush, sinking into the blackness. He leaned over, gazed into the shaft. And then he made a big mistake. He tried to stand, but the pebbly rocks beneath his feet offered no traction. He slipped, plummeting feet first into the mine. A blood-curdling scream followed, echoing through the shaft.

In seconds Willie reached the opening. He squealed his brother's name then listened, hoping to hear even the smallest indication that his brother was still alive, but he heard nothing. "Leonard, can ya hear me?"

Silence.

"Please Leonard, please! Say something! Anything! Let me know yer there."

Silence.

Tears streamed down Willie's cheeks, making his face feel sticky. He stood, still, unsure of what to do next. Should he stay—try to figure out how to get down the hole? He had no idea how deep it was. A few feet? A few hundred feet? A thousand? Did he leave his brother all alone and go for help? What if Leonard spoke and no one was there to hear him? He knew if he stayed, Leonard could die, if he wasn't dead already. A wave of guilt rushed over him.

Oh please, let him still be alive—please!

Five minutes ago, he'd have given anything to stop Leonard from asking any more questions, but now he'd give his own life just to hear his brother's tiny, angelic voice again.

Don't just stand here doing nothing, Willie. Think! What would Dad do?

He bent down and cupped his hands around both sides of his mouth. "Leonard, if ya can hear me, I'm goin' to get Mom and Dad. I'll be right back. I promise. I'm so…I'm so sorry. Ya hear me? I'm sorry…"

Willie sprinted toward his grandfather's house, his limbs experiencing an increasing burning sensation with every step. His entire body could burst into flames for all he cared—he'd risk anything to save his brother's life.

PRESENT DAY, 11:30 PM

Melody Sinclair hoisted a leg over the seat in front of her, slouched down, and scanned the room, eyeballing the men and women shuffling through the aisles of the old theater. Although each was unique in his or her own way, all of them displayed one distinct commonality: they were bundled up like they'd trekked through a blizzard to get here. January in Park City, Utah, had this effect on people. With outside temperatures dipping into the twenties and thirties, the majority of tourists in town for the annual Sundance Film Festival made haste. There was no escaping Old Man Winter. Not here.

Exuberant moviegoers took their seats, slowly shedding one layer of clothing after the other. Idle chatter began soon after, spreading through the air like the murmuring ripple of juicy gossip. Melody curled her long, blond hair around her index finger and savored every delicious second. This was her moment. Her fifteen minutes. Her time to shine.

It had been nearly a decade since Melody had submitted her first film for consideration at the festival. The film, a haunting recreation of the real-life horror that took place in the Hanley House back in the seventies, was sure to be a hit. At least in Melody's mind. The panel of esteemed judges saw it another way. *Haunting at Hanley House* was rejected and shelved, and per the festival rules, without significant changes, the film could never be resubmitted again. The rejection felt like an oversized, red stamp of disapproval. It meant the film wasn't good enough. It meant *she* wasn't good enough.

Distraught, Melody had almost decided to take her career in another direction. But that had all changed one night when she was approached by a dark, wavy-haired man at a movie after-party. His opening words to her had been, "I don't believe I've ever met a woman with eyes such a unique shade of green." At first she'd dismissed him, thinking it was nothing more than a cheap pickup line. But then her eyes met his bold, unwavering gaze.

He can't be serious. Can he?

The man's natural air of confidence commanded the room, even though his eyes locked on hers. "I'm Giovanni." She opened her mouth to speak, but he stopped her. "And you are Melody Sinclair."

She glanced down at his extended hand, noticing the shiny, oval-shaped ring on his pinkie finger. A semester in college studying Roman history taught her that signet rings worn on the pinkie finger had once symbolized power and authority. Whoever this man was, he definitely fit the bill.

"How did you know my name?" she asked.

"I know the names of all my guests, especially those who know my brother."

She waved the fluted glass of champagne in front of her, unaware that the single flick of her hand had caused the overpriced liquid to spill over. "Carlo is your brother? And this is...your house?"

An hour later the two sat side by side on a sofa in a private room. The conversation turned to the movie they'd seen that night, and Melody confessed she'd tried making her own film that year, a film she now referred to as an "epic failure."

"The great question is not whether you have failed, but whether you are content with failure," he'd encouraged her.

She giggled, running the tips of her fingers over her lips. "Did you come up with that yourself?"

He shook his head. "It's a Chinese proverb. You made one movie. It was unsuccessful. Make another. And *keep* making them until you achieve what you set out to accomplish in life."

Months after their brief encounter, a winter vacation led her to Park City, Utah, a thriving community that had once been an abandoned ghost town. Having been abandoned herself as a child, she felt right at home. And when one of the old-timers started chatting about the town's colorful history one evening at a local bar, she soon discovered Park City was much more than she realized. It wasn't just home to what had once been known as one of the world's richest silver mines—it was a town with a deadly past.

One year later Melody submitted a new film. *Bed of Bones* was accepted as one of eight "Park City at Midnight" films to be screened at the festival. And now here she was, mere moments away from watching her precious baby premiere in front of a sold-out crowd.

"I heard this film is based on a true story," a man who sat one row in front of her said to the ginger-haired woman next to him.

The woman let out an obnoxious noise that sounded more like a shrill cackle than anything else. She faced the man, the look on her face indicating she viewed him as a babbling imbecile. "Oh, I doubt it, Stuart. I've never heard of this kind of thing happening here. Not in Utah. You know how film makers are these days. They take one fact from history and weave ninety minutes of pure fiction around it to sell tickets. Nope. Never happened. I'm sure of it."

"It was over fifty years ago, Gladys," he responded. "You weren't alive then. How would you know?"

Gladys crossed her arms in front of her, plopped them down on her oversized belly, and hissed loud enough to make the elderly couple a few seats over glance in her direction. She jabbed Stuart with her elbow. "I wasn't around when Jack the Ripper hacked up all those half-naked ladies of the night either, but I know about him."

Stuart sighed, tipping his chin toward the ceiling, wondering why he'd bothered speaking in the first place.

A man resembling Tom Selleck back in his *Magnum, P.I.* days appeared on stage, his presence generating a titillating reaction from the females in the room. A wave of excitement ripped through the air until the women in the audience leaned a little closer to the edge of their seats. Then one by one, they all reclined back, realizing it was a false alarm. Whoever this man was, he wasn't Thomas Sullivan Magnum IV. The man flattened a hand over his forehead like he was saluting and eyeballed the crowd.

Melody glanced at the man sitting next to her. "That's my cue. Thanks for being here for me today, Giovanni."

Giovanni smiled and placed a hand on her leg, his pinkie ring noticeably absent. "Anything for a friend."

Melody exited the theater through the back-door, taking the hidden corridor on the side that led to the stage. The passageway was narrow and dark. Melody swished a hand from side to side in front of her, attempting to maneuver her way through the darkness. A faint noise vibrated in the distance. It sounded like a tin can being kicked on a concrete floor. "Hello, is someone there?"

The noise stopped.

Melody kept moving.

Then she heard something different.

Tick.

Tick.

Tick.

Melody stopped.

"Hello? Is someone there?"

A firm hand reached through the darkness, gripped her right arm, and squeezed. She gasped, jerking her hand back. She had an overwhelming urge to run. But where? And why? Who was this person, and why had he tried to place a stronghold on her arm?

A deep, male voice penetrated the pitch black passageway. "Right this way, Miss Sinclair." A flashlight clicked on, leading her out of the veil of darkness toward the stage. When she reached the safety of the stairs, the man released her. She turned, wanting to ask him about the strange noise she'd just heard, but it was too late— he'd faded back into the darkness. The Tom Selleck look-alike caught a glimpse of her out of the corner of his eye and said, "And now I'm pleased to present the director

and screenwriter of *Bed of Bones*, Melody Sinclair."
Although rattled, she knew the show must go on. He
nodded, passed her the mike, and backed away. The
audience applauded. She stepped forward, making sure
not to walk *too* fast. She'd never forgive herself if she
tripped now. The piercing glow from the strobe light
overhead zeroed in on her place on the stage, where she
stood, nervous inside. In seconds, the clapping ceased,
and the room quieted to a low hum.

Melody reached into her blazer pocket, her fingers
fumbling around for her glasses. They weren't there. She
cleared her throat and held the mike in front of her. "It's
an honor to be here today with all of you. Many years
ago, I contemplated giving up filmmaking forever. Then
someone gave me a piece of advice that stayed with me
to this day, and I learned it's never too late to achieve
your dreams. To the film students in the audience…no
matter how many times you fail in this business, keep
trying. Never lose your passion—it's the driving force
that makes life worth living."

A generous applause sounded from all sides of the
room. Not the thunderous roar an actor hears when their
name is read for an Academy Award, but to Melody, it
was no different. She paused, wishing she could hone in
on the red-haired skeptic for the final words of her
speech.

"The film you are about to see is based on a true story, as most of you already know from reading the introduction in your programs. But what most of you don't know is how true to life it really is. Many of you are used to fiction being weaved in with fact, lines being blurred, with no way of knowing the truth when you see it. You won't find that here. Not today. And so I implore you. After the film ends, and the lights come up, and you're wondering if what you've just witnessed really did happen the way it was portrayed in the movie…go home, get on your computer, and do some research of your own. Or come up and ask me yourself at the director's table. Either way, discover the truth for yourselves, and let the truth set you free. I want to thank everyone for coming out today. Enjoy the movie."

It was just how she'd rehearsed it, exactly how she'd planned. She flicked the microphone off, set it on the podium, and exited stage right. The lights dimmed, and the movie began. When Melody reached the other side of the corridor, her assistant was waiting. "Great job out there."

Melody smiled. "You should be inside, watching the movie."

"I wanted to be the first to congratulate you."

Melody placed a hand on her arm. "It means a lot, Brynn. Thank you. Now get in there. I don't want you to miss it!"

"What about you? Aren't you coming?"

"In a minute. I can't find my glasses. I thought they were in my pocket. They're not. I must have left them in the car."

"I'll get them for you," Brynn said. "You'll miss the beginning."

Melody shook her head. "Go. I'll be right behind you."

The chill of night nipped at Melody's face when she pushed open the theater door, causing a numbing sensation to come over her. She wrapped her sweater tightly around her and increased her pace, thankful her car was parked nearby. An overhead light streamed through the front windshield. The glasses were not on the dash. She opened the car door and paused.

Tick.

Tick.

Tick.

The familiar noise was close. One thing was certain—it was the same sound she'd heard inside. A watch perhaps? No, too loud. She considered reversing back into her car and locking herself in, but there was no time. She didn't know how she knew. She just did. She inhaled a crisp breath of air and turned around.

Not more than two feet in front of her was a person she assumed to be a man. He wore a ski mask. It was black, frayed at the edges. It looked like it had been sliced with a knife to make it shorter, but it still got the job done. *But what was the job?* Was he braving the elements, or did he pose some kind of threat?

When the giant rubber boots he was wearing stepped forward, she didn't know whether to laugh or cry, or both. She'd heard of people getting mugged or worse in big cities, but here? She never thought it was possible. She scanned the parking lot. Not a soul was in sight. Everyone was inside. She glanced at the theater door. Brynn wasn't there. No one was. She was alone.

"I—I don't have any money. My purse is inside."

He grunted. "Don't want your money."

"Are you here for the movie? I have an extra ticket."

An extra ticket? Of course he wasn't blocking her for an extra ticket. She had no idea what to say, and somehow she persuaded herself if she kept talking, she'd talk her way out of whatever this was. Talking had gotten her out of plenty sticky situations in the past.

"I…ahh…need to get back inside," she stuttered.

"Why? What's the rush?" His voice was low and controlled. His movements slow and confident.

"People are waiting for me."

"Why?"

"This is my movie. I directed it. And if I don't get back inside, they'll come out here looking for—"

"That so?" A lump of black liquid shot through the mouth opening of the mask. Tobacco juice drizzled onto her shoe. "Don't see anyone coming for you now."

"If you don't get out of my way, I'll...I'll...scream."

He shrugged. "What's stopping you?"

She clenched her jaw. *Whatever you do, don't panic. Don't let him see your fear.* But her usual charm wasn't working, and she was out of things to say. Aside from his crude demeanor, he hadn't touched her and he hadn't threatened her. She took it as a good sign. "Are you here for the movie? I can get you in."

He cocked his head to the side and let it hang there. "All I care about is the ending."

"What ending?"

"Yours."

Tick.

Tick.

Tick.

And then...*ding.*

The man opened his hand. Crushed inside were her glasses. He curved his hand sideways, letting them fall, smiling as he caught the stunned reaction on her face. Then he dug into his pocket, pulled out a small, square box. It appeared to be made of plastic. He pressed a grey button in the center. And the theater exploded.

CHAPTER 2

TWO HOURS LATER

I could count on one hand the number of times Park City Police Chief Wade Sheppard had dialed my number over the last year, so when his name flashed across my cell phone screen in bright, white letters, I paused, then glanced at the time. It was just after two a.m.

"Sloane?" he croaked, when I answered. His voice was shaky, unstable. Very unlike him. "I apologize for calling so late. How's Vegas?"

"Vegas is fine. What's wrong?"

"I need to ask you about Giovanni," he said. "When's the last time you talked to him?"

Giovanni Luciana, with whom I'd recently presumed not only shared a bed with me, but also the mafia, had been my on-again, off-again boyfriend for more than a year. At present, we were off-again. Sort of. It was complicated.

"I talked to him a few days ago," I said. "Why?"

"On the phone or in person?"

"On the phone. Why?"

"And when did you see him last?" he prodded.

"A couple weeks, maybe more. *Why?*"

"Are you two still together?"

The late-night interrogation session grated on me. I imagined Giovanni lying dead in the street, a single gunshot wound to the head, fired from a fancy shotgun equipped with silencer. I knew it was wrong to go there, but I couldn't help it. In my dreams, his life always ended the same way—with him brutally murdered. Dreams had a way of messing with a person's mind, projecting every day fears into some sort of twisted reality. At least all of mine did.

The chief had gone quiet, probably a result of my failure to answer his last question.

"Are you still there?" I asked.

He coughed like he had something lodged in his throat. In all the years I'd known him, he'd never been at a loss for words before.

"Look, we're not seeing other people," I said, "but we're not seeing a lot of each other right now either. It's hard to explain." Only, it wasn't. The chief knew it and I knew it, and I'd long speculated the chief was aware of Giovanni's extracurricular activities too. He'd never said a word—not to me or Giovanni. But whenever he got the chance, he pressed me about our relationship. And he wasn't asking for nothing.

"Are you with Madison right now?" he asked.

"Yeah, Maddie's sitting right here."

To my right, Maddie sat, legs crossed, donning a coral satin spaghetti-strapped top and matching shorts. She'd given her long, blond hair a reprieve for the night, taking it out of its usual pigtails, allowing her shoulder-length bangs to fall over her eyes. She took a sip of red wine, uncrossed her legs, and swapped the glass for an open bottle of glittery, pink nail polish on the nightstand. We made eye contact, and she mouthed something to me that at first sounded like, "Hut's going long." I deciphered it to mean, "What's going on?" Since no actual words came out of her mouth, I couldn't be sure, but there weren't any huts in Las Vegas to my knowledge, and neither of us was going long tonight. When I mouthed back that the chief was on the phone, she set the polish down and reached her hand out, taking the phone from me.

"Babe, what's happening?" she said into the phone.

This was followed by dead silence. "Babe" talked and Maddie listened, her face morphing into a series of different looks ranging from concerned to something she rarely expressed: genuine fear. Every few seconds, she'd glance my way and fake a smile, trying to convince me everything was okay. It didn't work. It never worked. We'd been friends for over twenty years. At this point, I didn't miss much. One more quick glance my way and Maddie said, "I understand." Then she ended the call.

"What did you hang up?" I asked. "We weren't finished talking."

She reached over, placing a hand on top of mine. I yanked it back.

"Okay," I said. "Now you're scaring me. What's going on?"

"We need to go home."

"When?"

"Now."

"We just got here," I said. "What's happened?"

She paused, her eyes shifting to the ceiling fan swirling above us.

"Not you too, Maddie. I expect the silent treatment from him, but not from you."

"There's been an accident."

"Where?"

"At home—at the film festival."

Ever since the chief had started dating Maddie, he had, in my opinion, tried to make her services exclusive to the Summit County Police Department any time a coroner was required. Problem was, she was the favorite ME of many departments in the surrounding counties.

This gave her more work than she could handle, and little free time. "There are other MEs he can call besides you. We're on vacation."

She tossed the phone back to me. "It's not what you think."

With my hands on my hips, I said, "It isn't? He called my phone intentionally, and now I know why. He planned to sweet talk me into cutting this trip short, but when I answered, he felt guilty. And when he didn't know what to say, he asked all these random questions about Giovanni. Am I right? Because if I am, he can—"

"Sloane," she said, her voice raised. "Listen to me. There was an explosion at one of the theaters tonight." She glanced at the time. "Well, last night. Two or three hours ago."

"Which theater?"

"He didn't say."

"By explosion you mean…"

"They think someone planted a bomb or multiple bombs. Wade doesn't have a lot of information yet. He said he'd call again when he knows more. We need to go home."

I stood up and pressed my hands together, slowly raising them to my scorching-hot face. "Of course." A bomb. In Park City. During the biggest event of the year. I didn't want to believe it was true. "Why was he asking about Giovanni? Does he think Giovanni can help in some way? Even if we haven't spoken much lately, I can still give him a call."

"I don't know how else to say this so I'm just going to say it," she said. "He was in the theater when the explosion happened."

"Who was?"

"Giovanni."

I shook my head. "Impossible. Giovanni's in New York. He doesn't come back until—"

She rested a hand on my shoulder. "No, Sloane. He's not."

"I don't believe it. He would have called me when he got back into town. We were supposed to talk."

"It's him. Wade verified he was at the theater."

"With who?"

She frowned, then shrugged.

I attempted to lift my suitcase off the ground and rest it on the edge of the bed. It was empty, but felt like it had been weighted down with a ton of bricks.

"Here, let me help you," Maddie said.

"How bad was the explosion? Any fatalities?"

"Two so far."

I sat back down, my head swirling in sync with the ceiling fan above me. "Is he...umm...I mean...did the chief say whether Giovanni is...umm..."

Maddie sat next to me, slinging an arm around my neck. "I don't know, sweetie. Let's hope not."

CHAPTER 3

My mind was wandering again. With Maddie behind the wheel, it wasn't hard to drift off. She'd said little since we'd left Las Vegas, and usually I couldn't get her to *stop* talking. The last time I'd seen Giovanni, we argued, something I regretted now. The two of us had been out to dinner together, and I had prodded him, in a gentle way, for information about his sister. He'd remained tight-lipped, and did what he always did when I said something he didn't like—he changed the subject. I'd let it slide in the past, but not this time.

Giovanni's sister, Daniela, had been kidnapped a few months earlier, and yet somehow, he'd managed to find, rescue, and return her home within a week—*without* involving the police. As a private investigator, I knew damn well the average person never had much success finding a missing person on his own—that's why they came to me, or the police, or in some cases, both. But Giovanni wasn't anything like the average person.

At the time of Daniela's kidnapping, a handful of Giovanni's men went on the rescue mission, but not all of them came back. Yet another topic he wouldn't discuss. And I'd grown tired of all the secrecy.

I'd gotten up and tossed my napkin on the table, attempting to storm out in true diva fashion. I thought I would make it to the door unscathed, my point proven, but it was always moments like this when I made the stupidest mistake of all. As I sauntered away from him, nose held high, the heel of my strappy, black shoe caught in between two tiles on the floor where the grout had chipped away, and my heel broke off in the crack. This only furthered my embarrassment. Not only was *he* looking at me, everyone else was too. One less-than-gracious woman even giggled behind a napkin she'd masked in front of the lower half of her face. I ditched the heel and did exactly what my anxiety suggested: I kicked the other heel off my foot, grabbed the remaining three quarters of my other shoe, and ran, leaving the heel behind. I wasn't proud of myself for putting on such a ridiculous charade, but I couldn't keep giving up so much of myself and getting so little in return, no matter how wonderful he treated me.

For us to work, I needed him to let me in, and even if by some miracle he did, could I really look the other way while he lived a shady lifestyle just because he was good to me? I'd looked the other way when I suspected him of murdering his sister's former lover. I'd looked the other way when he shot two bullets into Sam Reids' skull while I was in the next room. In both cases, I allowed myself to believe the deaths were justified. Daniela's lover had beaten her on more than one occasion and threatened her life. Serial killer Sam Reids had kidnapped and murdered a handful of women, my sister included.

They both got what they deserved in the end.

Hadn't they?

Maddie looked at me and winked. "I was going to say 'penny for your thoughts,'" she said. "But for yours, I'd offer at least a quarter. Maybe even two."

"Trust me; you're better off not knowing."

"Do you want to make a quick pit stop? Use the ladies room or grab a donut...use the ladies room *and* grab a donut?"

I glanced at her.

"Didn't think so," she said. "It's not much longer anyway."

Since we left, I'd tried calling Giovanni's right-hand man, Lucio, every fifteen minutes. Four hours and sixteen calls later, he still hadn't answered, and my OCD had officially gone into overdrive.

I pulled the visor down and flipped open the mirror. Strands of my long, usually lustrous, straight, black hair, were stuck to the side of my face, like they'd been hair sprayed in place. I picked them off, using my fingers to comb them to the side. My mascara was gone, but even without it I could always count on my sparkly, brown eyes to brighten things up, especially when the rest of me was falling apart. "What reason would a person have to bomb a theater in Park City?"

Maddie looked over. "You know as well as I do this type of thing can happen anywhere at any time. There are a lot of crazy people out there."

"Yeah, but Park City seems so low risk."

"Think about it. Columbine, Oklahoma City, Newtown. Most of these places never make national news otherwise."

"I was just thinking…"

"That's your first mistake."

"What—trying to figure things out?" I asked.

"I was leaning toward your lack of patience. There's nothing *to* figure out. We don't have all the details yet."

I slumped back in the seat. Maybe she was right. If only there was a kill switch, something to put my brain on hold a little longer.

After a few minutes passed, Maddie began gnawing on the inside of her mouth.

"What is it?" I asked.

"Nothing."

"It's something. You're biting your lip."

She sighed. "Out of curiosity, what *were* you thinking?"

"I imagine there are a lot of people out there who want Giovanni dead."

CHAPTER 4

The statement was true. You don't get to the top of the mafia food chain without making a significant number of enemies. Daniela wasn't snatched for no reason. Whoever took her wanted to send a message. It made me wonder what kind of message the theater bomber was sending, and to whom.

We arrived back in Park City a little after nine in the morning. As we neared the theater, two patrol cars became five, and then seven. The traffic headed out of town stretched as far as the eye could see. Cars ahead of us were being rerouted through a side street that weaved through a neighborhood in Prospector before spilling out a good distance away from the theater. Everyone was curious, and those who weren't were packing their bags, returning from whence they came.

When it was our turn, we weren't steered in another direction; we were stopped by the last person I wanted to see, Detective Drake Cooper, a man who, in his fifty-seven years of life, had spent half his time mulling over all the ways he'd been screwed over by everyone from the police chief to the checker at the local supermarket, and the other half doing something he actually excelled at: fighting crime. When he spotted my Audi, he flattened his hand in front of him like he was prepared to stop my car with it. He then circled his pointer finger in the air.

Maddie lowered the car window, but kept her eyes on the road.

Coop bent his six-foot-five frame down, poking his enlarged head inside. "Good morning to you too."

He wasn't smiling, per his usual.

"Let us pass, Coop," I said.

"Can't do that, sweetheart."

His tone dripped with sarcasm.

"What's wrong this time?"

"Only police personnel can be admitted to the scene. We're keeping things under wraps—you know the protocol."

"What *things?*"

"If I told you, it wouldn't be under wraps now, would it?"

"The chief called me personally," I said.

He rested a hand on his hip, mocking me. "What do you know—he called *me* personally today too."

"Maddie has clearance," I said.

"Not on this one, she doesn't."

Without the presence of the chief, we were gridlocked, a fact Coop relished. He thumped on the hood of the car with his fist. "If the chief wants to grant you two access to the scene, it's on his watch, not mine. Until then, back this thing up."

"Can you at least tell me where the chief is?"

"I'm not your errand boy. Call him yourself." Just as Maddie placed her finger on the button to put the window up, Coop added, "What are you doing here anyway, Sloane? Shouldn't you be at the hospital?"

Maddie smiled. "At least we know where Giovanni is now. Thanks, Coop."

He rolled his eyes. She jammed the car into reverse, spun around, and punched the gas, making a spectacle of herself as she peeled out. For a girl like Maddie, there wasn't any other way.

"You know," she began, "Coop's the type of guy that could turn a sane, rational person into a cold-blooded killer after a single conversation. And yet he saved your life awhile back." She swayed her head back and forth. "I'll never understand."

I did. It was his job. Nothing personal.

The chief's secretary, Mary, called Maddie on her cell phone. Mary said he'd been tied up all day. He asked Mary to arrange a meeting with us at the station later

today. Maddie pressed her for more information and
learned the joint terrorism task force was assembling a
team. Soon they'd be on their way to Park City.

I tried Lucio again. Still no answer. But now I knew
where Giovanni was, and I hoped, alive.

CHAPTER 5

Daniela was the first person I spotted after stepping through the revolving door of the Summit Medical Center in Heber. She rose from a chair, embraced me. I said, "How is he? What happened? Why was he even at the..." And then I stopped. One look at her tear-stained face, and I knew she was in no condition to answer my questions.

A knot jolted my stomach. The look on her face was one of loss. It couldn't be true. It just couldn't. I wanted to grab her, shake her. Scream.

Please let him be alive!

Instead, I held her and whispered, "Are you okay?"

She shook her head.

"What can I do to help?" I asked.

"Nothing." She picked a hair band out of her back pocket and whipped her long, dark locks into a loose bun. "How could this happen—to him of all people?"

Did she mean it? Surely, she had some indication of the kind of danger the family business put him in.

She aimed a polished, black fingernail at me. "I'm going to find whoever did this and make him understand what happens when you mess with a Luciana."

Spoken like a true Mafioso. I glanced at Maddie, who had spent the last two minutes beating the life out of the plastic panel on the soda vending machine with her clenched fist. She put the money in, the machine spit it back out. After several failed attempts, Maddie placed the dollar on her pants, ironing it flat. She prayed out loud to anyone listening for it to work and stuck the dollar back in so delicately, for a moment it was like the machine was a life-size version of the game Operation. This time, it didn't just spill back out, it shot out. She threw her hands in the air and glanced at Daniela. "I guess I didn't want soda after all. I'm going to find a cup of coffee. Want to join me?"

Except for engaging in idle chit chat at one or two of Giovanni's dinner parties, Maddie and Daniela hadn't spent much time around one another. In any other instance, Daniela would have refused the offer. But crisis mode changed people, often times opening the dusty, closed windows we all hide behind.

Daniela nodded. I tried not to show my astonishment.

Maddie passed me and whispered, "I'll stay with her. Go find him."

A game of hide-and-go-seek commenced wherein I dodged the hospital staff, snooping inside the staggered patient rooms as I made my way down the hall. I'd successfully crossed half a dozen off my list when someone tugged on the sleeve of my sweater. I stiffened.

"Going somewhere?"

The masculine voice was a familiar one. I turned, venting a sigh of relief.

"Carlo, I was hoping to see you here," I said. "Did you fly in to help with the investigation?"

Carlo had wavy, black hair, just like Giovanni, a strong but slender build, and the kind of tanned skin women went to the beach all summer long for. With his FBI status, I hoped he could provide me with some answers.

"It's not my department, but I've found a way to get involved. I will find out who did this to my brother."

I didn't doubt it.

"If you want to see Giovanni, I can take you to him," he continued.

"So, he's...alive?"

Carlo nodded. "Although, he hasn't been himself since I arrived."

"What do you mean?"

"He's unnerved," he said. "Shaken up."

"It's understandable after what he just experienced."

"All these years he's convinced himself he was untouchable. Invincible. Now he knows he isn't. That...changes a person. Whatever he says to you, try to understand he's processing a lot right now. It may take some time before he finds clarity."

I wasn't sure what Carlo was trying to say, or not say. His tone conveyed a warning of some kind, like Giovanni was a loose cannon, prepped and ready to fire. Part of me couldn't help feeling like it was exactly what we needed as a couple.

He tapped his expensive, leather shoe on the floor. "This can't get out...it just can't."

"What can't?"

I didn't know what I expected to accomplish with my question. Carlo was a Luciana. It wasn't like he would open up to me either.

In true brotherly fashion, he shifted the conversation. "I heard you two have been having some difficulties lately, but Giovanni didn't go into detail."

I wasn't about to either. In true girlfriend fashion, I changed the subject myself. "How badly is he hurt?"

He stepped back, a look of shock on his face. "You don't know?"

"No."

"What *do* you know?" he asked.

"I was told there was an explosion at one of the theaters in town—not much more. I tried calling Lucio several times. He never answered."

Carlo rested a hand on my shoulder. "Sloane, Lucio is dead."

Dead? I didn't want to believe it. Over the last year, I'd become fond of his oversized shadow tailing me wherever I went.

"What—how? He was there?"

"Lucio was sitting next to Giovanni when the explosion happened. To be honest, it's been hard getting more information out of my brother other than small, insignificant details. I'm hoping you'll be more successful."

We continued down the hall. "What *can* you tell me?"

"I can share what little we know so far. Witnesses who were there at the time confirmed the explosion happened right as the movie was starting, during the opening credits, before the opening scene."

"Do you know what types of explosives were used?"

He nodded.

"Fragments from pressure-cooker bombs were found near the stage."

"Bombs plural—as in more than one?"

"It's possible there were as many as three. Hard to say for sure right now. They're still gathering evidence."

"Have you pinpointed the exact location of the blast?" I asked.

"There was a table set up for the director and a few of the actors to take questions after the movie was over. It was blown to bits. Chief Sheppard thinks the bombs were hidden underneath. The table was in plain sight, but it was covered with a black cloth that went all the way to the floor. There was no reason for anyone to sit there until after the film was over."

"Any idea how the bombs were set off?"

"All we know is that they were close-controlled."

"I'm sorry…what?"

"Whatever device was used, it had to be relatively close to the theater in order to achieve the desired effect."

"I see," I said.

Carlo stopped. He faced me. "You don't have any idea what I'm talking about, do you?"

"Not really. I've never dealt with a bomb before."

He cupped one hand about six inches over the other like he was creating an invisible replication of the explosive device. "Shrapnel is placed inside of the pressure cooker. A lot of times they use a combination of gunpowder and nails, anything made of metal that is capable of inflicting the maximum amount of injuries. All of it is stuffed inside the pressure cooker and secured with a tight-fitting lid. The idea is that when it explodes, it will cause mass injury and death to as many people as possible. Because most people were sitting at the time of the explosion, the majority of injuries we're seeing are from the waist up."

"Any idea how many fatalities?"

"We don't have an exact body count yet. Three confirmed dead. They're still trying to account for everyone who was there at the time."

"I'm sorry about Lucio."

He shrugged. "I knew him, but not like my brother did. He's lost friends before, but not like this."

"I'm just glad Giovanni is alive."

Carlo turned and pointed. Positioned on both sides of the door to Giovanni's room were two men I didn't recognize. Both dressed in black, both bald, both looking like bouncers at a high-end nightclub. Carlo behaved as if the men weren't even there. The men stood, stiff like statues—one looked left, the other right. Neither looked at me. Carlo slanted his head toward the door then stepped back.

"You're not coming in?" I asked.

"I think it's best you see him alone. I'll be here if you need me."

I nodded and walked inside, pushing the door closed behind me like the room contained a baby I didn't want to wake. I was skittish, but I didn't know why. For a time I stood still, wondering what I would encounter when I regained my nerve long enough to round the corner.

What would he look like?

How bad was he hurt?

I stepped forward, the heel of my boot clacked along the vinyl floor, giving me away.

A hand reached out, firm and masculine, reeling the curtain back. "Nurse, I need you to bring me—"

"No, Giovanni. It's me."

He looked like he wanted to shield himself behind the curtain again.

"Sloane…I…you shouldn't be here."

Shouldn't be here?

I had every right to be there.

Most of Giovanni's body was covered with a thin, blue blanket, but his arms were exposed. They were hacked up, cut like someone had taken a blunt razor blade, slashing him numerous times. Positioned over his left eye was a thick piece of gauze with some clear tape over it. I walked to his side, choking back the tears. I didn't want to stare. I tried to look away, focus on anything else, but I couldn't. "Your eye, is it—"

Not one to mince words, he captured my hand inside his. "Gone, yes. I didn't want you to see me this way."

"What...happened?"

"It doesn't matter now," he replied.

"It does to me."

"I don't want you involved in this."

"It's too late. I'm here, and I am."

"I've spoken to Carlo. I've asked him to take you out of here—somewhere safe."

Funny, Carlo hadn't mentioned it to me.

I released his hand, drew a chair from the corner of the room, and sat next to the bed. "Why? What's happening?"

"I can explain more later. Right now you need to trust me."

"I won't be shipped off to some random location, especially when I don't understand why I'm going there in the first place."

"There's no point in arguing with me," he said.

"I'm not—we're talking."

"I must insist, Sloane. You *will* go. The arrangements are being made now. You'll leave tonight."

I *will* go?

It's what I'd always run from in the past—overbearing, controlling men. I thought he was different.

I thought he understood. "I care about you, but I don't and I won't take orders from you, or anyone."

"I can't protect you—not in here, not like this!"

He slammed a fist down on a wooden table beside him. A metal tray launched off the edge, clanking as it touched the ground. I reached down, picked it up, moved it to a safer location. Out of the corner of my eye, I saw Carlo peer around the corner while Giovanni wasn't looking. I cracked a smile, indicated I was fine. He backed away.

Finally, a taste of what it was like when Giovanni became angry. Up until now he'd always been so composed, civilized. I sat down again. "What do I need protecting from? Can you at least give me a name?"

He transferred his gaze to a blank wall.

Silence. Always silence.

"You can't even answer one question, can you?" I asked. "You just expect me to leave because you want me to—I'm not one of your lackeys."

I leaned forward in the chair, encircled my hands around the nape of my neck, and focused on the faded, grey flecks in the tiles below. The floor looked like it hadn't been replaced for several decades, if ever. How many had sat before me in the exact same spot I was sitting now, praying for a loved one, clinging to faith, hoping for a miracle?

"I wouldn't ask you to go if it wasn't necessary," he said.

"You didn't ask. You told me. Why is it necessary?"

"I've always respected your judgment in the past. Now you need to respect mine."

Hospitals scared me, but not as much as the icy chill I felt at this moment. He'd never been so cold before. "I'm…not…going…anywhere without an explanation."

Judging by the look on his face, I prepared for a second explosion of major proportions. I wanted to meet his hardened glare, but I couldn't. Not because of his anger—because of my guilt. It wasn't easy sitting in front of him, seeing him tired and sluggish, like a…regular person. Gone was the debonair suit, the fifty-thousand-dollar watch, the kind, gentle man I'd come to know. Sitting in front of me was a man consumed by hate.

This was his other side.

The one I'd never seen.

The one I always thought I needed to see.

Except now I wished I hadn't.

CHAPTER 6

It was over three full minutes before Giovanni spoke again. I knew the exact timing because, while I waited, I watched the seconds tick by on a worn, chipped, metal clock dangling from a rusty nail on the wall in front of me. Every so often, I snuck a peek, watching him wrestle inwardly with his feelings, his face expressing a strange combination of sorrow, anger, hurt, and rage. I watched and waited, hoping in the end, the man who addressed me next would be a lot more Dr. Jekyll than Mr. Hyde.

He sat up straighter, ogling me with a one-eyed stare down. His face had softened, a little. Part of me wanted to embrace him, but the thought of his possible rejection kept me glued to the chair.

"Before we met," he said, "I hadn't been in a serious relationship in six years. Because of what I do for a living, which I trust you know, I didn't believe I could be with a woman and keep her safe. Every woman I've ever known, aside from my mother, needed saving, until I met you. Strong, independent, and as tough as nails—at least when you want to be. In many ways, I'd met my equal. In others, I'd met my opposite. The combination of the two fueled my attraction when we first met. I admire your desire for justice. You always want to do what's right. It hasn't been easy, watching you struggle within yourself over the life I lead. At times, it's pained you—the secrets, the life I never shared."

Carlo was right. Giovanni's behavior was unusual. There was an air of nostalgia in his words, followed by an air of regret. "Is there something you're trying to tell me?"

"It's…my fault. It's *all* my fault."

"What is?"

"The explosion, my sister's kidnapping—all of it."

"How can you be so sure? They haven't found the person responsible for the explosion yet."

"There are things I cannot say. Not right now."

His tone suggested there would come a time when he told me everything I wanted to know. Too bad I didn't believe it.

"Let me in, Giovanni. Trust me. Please."

His face changed and I understood. It wasn't about not trusting me, and it wasn't about not letting me in. It was trepidation over how I would view him once I crossed over to the other side, finally understanding the entire scope of how he lived. Even after a year together, it was still a risk he wasn't willing to take.

I stood. "I'm not sure what's happening or why you're so afraid, but I need to stay."

There was no rebuttal this time, no trying to convince me otherwise. He looked at me like he hadn't expected anything less, even though he knew he needed to try.

"Please don't be disappointed," I continued. "You've always looked out for me whether I've been aware of it or not, and I am grateful for everything we've been through together. But I can't run. I can't hide. I just can't. Whatever this is…I need to see it through."

He reached out, pulled me toward him. We kissed, and I tried to deny feeling like we were embracing for the last time.

"I love you, Sloane. You will always be a part of me." He cupped his hands around my face. "There are a few matters I must attend to when I leave here. There's a good possibility I'll be away for a while. I believe it would be best for us to—"

He choked back the words.

"To what?" I asked.

He looked away.

"Giovanni, please."

"It would be best if you didn't see me anymore."

CHAPTER 7

"Do you want to talk about it?" Maddie squirmed in the passenger seat of the car, trying to get comfortable.

"About what?"

"Whatever happened at the hospital just now? You look like you've been stricken with a deadly virus. I talked to Daniela. Her brother lost an eyeball—so what? He's going to be fine. He'll get one of those glass eyes, and I tell you what, I'll bet it makes him even hotter."

"I'm not worried about his eye," I said.

"What did he say to you?"

"He thinks the explosion is his fault—like someone has a personal vendetta against him and his family."

"And they'd blow up an entire building, injuring and killing innocent people, because of it?"

I shrugged. "He thinks everyone he cares about is in danger right now—including me."

"What about Carlo? What did he have to say?"

"Nothing. He didn't say one thing about a personal connection. He confirmed a few people had died and said pressure-cooker bombs were responsible for the blast. It doesn't make any sense."

Maddie tipped her head to the side. "Sometimes it never does."

...

The outside of the police station was impregnated with men in suits when we arrived. The suits were black. The shirts were white, button-up. The ties were navy, maroon, or black—muted—nothing flashy. From the neck down, they looked like adults wearing the same school-assigned uniform. No personality, no sign of individuality anywhere. I hoped for a hot-pink sock, a diamond-stud earring, anything to suggest there was even one renegade within the organization. I settled with disappointment.

The chief stopped us in front of his pickup truck before we parked the car.

"I thought we were meeting in your office," I said.

"Best we talk out here. Too much corn inside."

"Corn?"

"You know—ears. People listening."

"Any updates?" I asked.

"A fourth fatality has just been confirmed, two others are in critical, and we've still got a few dozen injuries, most from those sitting closest to the stage. The chairs absorbed about half of the blast or we'd be dealing with a lot more."

"And the pressure-cooker bombs," I said. "Have they been confirmed?"

"From what we can piece together, there were three. Damn things shot shards of metal out as fast as bullets. Some of the victims had over thirty pieces of shrapnel stuck in them." He raised a brow. "How do you know about the bombs? Have you been to see Giovanni?"

Even the sound of his name pained me. "Carlo."

"Special Agent Luciana. Figures. What else did he say?"

"Not much. Any suspects?"

"The task force thinks we're dealing with a terrorist group."

"Based on what? This isn't New York City."

"The festival is a big deal, Sloane. You've got people flying in from all over, from multiple countries, celebrities, media coverage. Who knows how many other buildings might be targeted. We've got tourists leaving here in droves, most of the films have been shut down, and airport security is on high alert."

"I understand taking precautions, but until you have a better idea of the person or group you're dealing with—"

"There's no way to know right now. We're talking to everyone who was near the building for any reason over the past several days. So far we've got nothing. No one saw anything. We've got a few people of interest based on their backgrounds, but to be honest, I think they'll all check out."

Maddie, who up to this time had been silent, spoke up. "So when do I get access to the bodies?"

The chief sighed. "You don't, hun. I'm sorry."

"Isn't that why you called me back?"

"I did everything I could to stall, but they couldn't wait."

"They *wouldn't* wait is what you mean to say, right?"

"Madison, you know I want you in on this."

"Who'd you give it to—who's the ME?"

"Katherine Gellar."

"Kate's good, but she's not me," Maddie stated, arms crossed.

For a moment the chief forgot where he was—his lips brushed across Maddie's cheek. "No one is."

"Will I see you later?" she asked.

"I hope so."

"Is there any chance I can take a look at the scene?" I asked.

He frowned. "That's the other reason we're out here and not in there. I know this is like an itch you just gotta scratch, but I need you to stay away from this. We're handling it. With the task force here, you can't come barging into my office like you usually do when you want something. Understand?"

"But I——"

"No, Sloane, and that's final."

CHAPTER 8

No was one of those words that practically begged defiance. The first time I remember hearing it uttered to me was at the tender age of six. I asked for a bicycle. My father laughed at my request, shutting down my dream because we didn't "have enough money." What he should have said was we didn't have the money because he spent it all on booze whenever he wasn't working, and I doubted he clocked more than twenty hours a week.

Racked with guilt over the rejection, my mother helped me set up a lemonade stand by the street sign at the top of the hill. She even helped me color it. I drew yellow lemons across the top and bottom and gave each lemon a happy face. I thought if people driving by saw the smiley faces, it would make them happy, and then they'd buy my lemonade.

After sitting outside all day, every day, for two weeks, I'd finally earned enough money. That night I counted it all up, making sure I had just the right amount. Then I put it in a clear Mason jar and set in on my nightstand. I drifted off to sleep dreaming of popping wheelies and putting playing cards in the spokes of the bicycle wheel like all the other kids did.

It wasn't to be.

The next morning I woke to find an empty jar on my nightstand. A note scribbled with a dull pencil was crumpled in front, waiting for me. It said: IOU, Dad.

Funny thing about IOUs.

Some people don't have any intention of paying them back.

My dad was one of those people.

Still a bikeless wonder, the next summer I walked my elderly neighbor's dog every day before sundown. She paid me ten dollars a week. I cut a slit in the lining of my bedroom curtains with my father's carpenter's knife and stuffed the money inside. A few nights I caught him stumbling into my room before bed and muttering "son of a bitch" when he stumbled back out. When I went in after him, some of my dolls and stuffed animals had been strewn about, but he hadn't touched the drapes. He wasn't smart enough. Or sober enough. Or both.

He never found the money.

And four weeks later, I bought my bike.

With the extra law enforcement in town, there were too many suits milling around for me to sneak over to the scene—at least for now. I'd have to start

somewhere else and without the assistance of Maddie. I
wasn't the only one who'd be sitting this one out.

• • •

When I rounded the corner for home, I observed a faint
glow radiating through the vertical blinds in my living
room, casting a ray of light onto the wood decking on my
back porch. There was only one problem with this
scenario: thanks to my overwhelming desire to conserve
energy, I never left anything more than a front porch
light on when I wasn't home. Not ever.

I considered Giovanni's warning earlier that day,
but I still didn't want to believe it.

Was I in denial?

Could it be true?

Was someone after him, and, more importantly,
had they come for me?

My concern escalated when the living room light
flickered off for a moment and then back on again like a
lighthouse sending an accidental signal. Only it wasn't a
signal at all—it was a human shadow crossing the room.

Panic gripped me.

I'd left my Westie with a neighbor while I was
supposed to be vacationing in Vegas, but when I spoke to
her earlier in the day, she said she'd put him in my
bathroom while she went shopping in Salt Lake City with
her sister. It was just after nine o'clock. I called her. She

was still at the mall, and she hadn't left any lights on in my house.

If an intruder *was* in the house, why wasn't he barking?

I swallowed, forcing myself not to assume the worst. I couldn't. Not yet.

I switched my headlights off and coasted to a stop. Without taking my eyes off the back porch window, I eased my hand down the side of the car door, lifting my 9mm semi-automatic from the pocket. I pulled back on the slide, racking a round into the chamber.

In seconds I'd made it to the side of the house. With my back firmly pressed against the wood exterior, I inched my way over until I'd reached the edge. I drew my gun and poked my head around the corner.

I saw no one.

But I heard humming.

Someone was humming the tune of a song I'd never heard before. Whether the voice was male or female, I couldn't tell. I eased the back door open with the tips of my fingers, stepped inside, and aimed.

CHAPTER 9

With my free hand, I flipped the switch on the wall while holding the gun steady in front of me. Light illuminated the room. The petite frame in front of me swaying her hips from side to side was female, but in a baseball cap, and with her backside to me, it was impossible to assess her age.

I yanked the earplugs from her ears.

"Face me and put your hands where I can see them," I demanded.

She didn't turn around.

I cleared my throat. "I asked you to face me. Do it. Now."

She turned around, hands held partially in the air, fingers curled toward me, zombie style. She wore a jean mini skirt and a t-shirt tight enough to get her a job as a HOOTERS girl.

I gasped. "Shelby?"

"Can I put my hands down now or are you plannin' on makin' a citizen's arrest?"

She flung her head back and snorted a laugh.

Shelby McCoy was the daughter of a detective I'd worked with a few months earlier on a missing children's case I helped solve in Wyoming. She was rude and obstinate, and even worse, a teenager. We didn't get along.

"How did you get in here?" I said.

"You left a key to the house on the back porch."

"I most certainly did not."

She pointed. "Uh, yeah, you did."

"How did you—"

"Find it?" she cut in. "Under the doormat—too obvious. Over the door frame—too predictable. But taped to the inside of the broken knob on your barbeque grill? Now that's clever. I have to admit, it took me over five minutes, but..." she said, digging inside her pocket and dangling it in front of me on the tip of her pointer finger, "here it is. Ta-da."

I pointed toward the sofa, unamused. "Sit."

"Or what—you'll call the cops?"

"Why don't we start by calling your father? I'm guessing he doesn't know you're here, or I would have had some kind of warning by now. Now sit."

"Put the gun down."

"Sit," I repeated.

"Only if you put the gun down first. It's freaking me out. Seriously."

I released the hammer slowly, putting the pistol on safety before depositing it onto the counter. Shelby sat on the edge of the sofa, one butt cheek on, one teetering off. She glared at me as if she'd bolt if she didn't like what I was about to say.

"Where's my dog?" I asked.

She whistled.

Lord Berkeley bounded around the corner, collar jingling, bone clenched between his teeth. Today he'd received a big, fat F in the subject of owner protection.

"Cute dog. What's her name?"

"Lord Berkeley," I said. "Sometimes Boo."

"Your dog has two names?"

"Boo's a nickname."

"Oh I get it, because she's white."

"He."

"Well, *he* tried to eat me when I opened the door," she said, pointing. "Good thing I had a granola bar in my pocket."

A granola bar?

"How did you know where I live?" I asked.

"Your return address was on the card you sent my grandmother after my grandfather died."

"What are you doing here?"

"My dad kicked me out."

I doubted there was any truth to her statement.

"What did you do?" I asked.

"Nothing."

"Lie to me again, and I'll kick you out too."

She rolled her eyes so far back inside her head, all I could see were the whites. "All right." She flopped her body into a slouched position on the sofa, joined her fingers behind her head, and sighed with dramatic flair. "I've been, ahh, seein' this guy Jace for a few weeks. He's so nice. And cute. And—"

"Still doesn't explain what you're doing here."

"I'm getting to it, geez."

Only she wasn't. She was stalling.

"Last week he kind of got arrested for doing drugs."

How do you 'kind of' get arrested?

"And umm…my dad was the one who busted him," she continued. "Cuffed him right in front of me."

Good for him.

"My dad said I couldn't see Jace again as long as I was under his roof, which is really my grandmother's roof while we're building a house. I tried to tell him that, but…"

"So you left? Where's your car?"

She bobbed her shoulders up and down. "Don't have one."

"Then how did you get here?"

"I…umm…hitched."

"You thumbed a ride?" I asked.

"Two rides. Why not?"

"And your dad thinks you're where exactly?"

She shrugged.

"Are you telling me you haven't talked to him since you left?" I asked.

She stared down at her sparkly, pink Converse. "I was hopin' you could…you know…talk to him for me."

"And say what?"

"Convince him to give Jace another chance." She pressed her hands together like she was summoning a miracle from the Almighty. "Pretty please?"

It was the nicest she'd ever been to me. Actually, when I thought about it, it was the only time she'd ever been pleasant to me before. She wanted something, and as soon as she got it, she'd revert back into an ignorant teenager again. I shook my head. "I don't think so. And you shouldn't be here."

She squeezed her eyes shut in frustration. "You have to talk to him! He'll listen to you."

"Is that why you came here, so I could sweet-talk your father on your behalf?"

She grinned. "I wouldn't have come if I didn't think you could help me."

"I can't help you."

"Yes, you can. Ever since you left, you're all he talks about."

Was she turning on the charm, or was there a shred of truth in her words?

Except for the occasional text message, I hadn't spoken to her father in over two months. And even then, we kept things civil—asking how one another were doing, what cases we were working on, the usual. Every once in a while I thought back to the awkward moment we shared while working on the missing children's case together. We had been at the table contemplating our next move. He went in for a kiss, and I backed away, admitting I had another man in my life.

At present, I didn't know what I had anymore.

I sat on a chair next to the sofa. "I get it. Right now you think this guy, Jason—"

"Jace," she corrected.

"*Jace* is your whole world. Nothing I say will convince you he's not. So, here's the deal. I'll let you stay for a few nights *if* you call your father."

She opened her mouth. I raised a finger. She clamped it shut again.

"You *will* call him," I said. "You'll tell him you're here with me so he'll know you're safe."

She crossed her arms. "And if I don't?"

"There's the door," I gestured. "You can use it anytime."

She squinted. "You won't kick me out."

"Excuse me?"

"You won't."

"Why wouldn't I?" I asked.

"You're too nice."

If she really believed that, she didn't know me at all.

CHAPTER 10

Cade McCoy answered on the first ring. His breathing was frantic, agitated. "Sloane, I can't talk right now. Shelby's—"

"Here," I said. "Your daughter's here. And she's fine."

"What? What the hell's she doing—"

"She's in the shower. I've talked her into calling you when she gets out, but I'd rather she didn't know I spoke to you first. I think it's best if she handles it on her own, or at least thinks she's handling it on her own."

"Of all the places she could have run off to, I never thought she'd show up there. Look, I'm sorry. I never meant to get you involved."

"Don't be."

"Wait just a minute. How'd she get there?"

It was a question I had no desire to answer. She was in enough trouble already.

"Why don't you talk to her about that when she calls?" I said.

This way, I figured, he'd yell into the phone at her, instead of me.

"Shelby's just goin' through some stuff right now, and without her mother here, I'm at a loss. No matter what I do, she hates me."

"She doesn't, trust me. You're a good father, Cade. She's just a hormonal teenager."

"Yeah, well, I don't do 'hormonal teenager' very well."

I didn't know of any parent who did.

"I'm glad she came to me instead of putting herself in danger somewhere else. There's a lot going on right now, but if being here keeps her away from this Jace guy, it might be best for her to relax here for a few days while she works through everything."

"You'd do that—really?"

"I might not have a lot of experience with kids, but I have plenty in the wrong-kind-of-guy department."

"Sounds like things have…changed since we talked last?"

He was fishing. He must have detected my disgusted tone.

"I don't know," I said. "I'm too busy dealing with what's happening here."

"I saw it on the news. Are you involved?"

"Two people I care about were in the theater when it happened. One lost an eye, the other, his life. I'd like to think the police or the feds or whoever else they bring in will find the person responsible, but you know me—hard to sit back and do nothing."

"It's only been one day. Have some faith in the system."

Spoken like a true officer of the law.

"Don't take this on yourself, Sloane. Promise me."

The water in the shower lulled to a stop. "She's out," I whispered. "I have to go."

"Sloane, wait."

"Yeah?"

"Keep me updated. And please, be careful."

CHAPTER 11

The phone rang a full five times before I answered it. Six and it would have gone to voicemail. In the few seconds I sat staring at the name on the caller ID, I couldn't decide what I wanted to do—talk to him or let him leave a message. He'd just call again. I knew that.

"Giovanni, I—"

The phone clicked.

Maybe he thought I hadn't answered, or maybe he heard me and decided he had nothing to say. I called back. It rang. No answer, no voicemail, nothing.

I was still shaken up from our conversation earlier. Part of me wanted to cry, another part of me was relieved. All of me wanted to get off the fence.

Boo hopped off the bed, teeth clenched, in full growl mode.

What now?

"What is it?"

All four paws scampered toward the front door. I wasn't in the mood for another unexpected visitor. For the second time tonight, I reached for my gun, even though I had serious doubts about how capable I was of shooting something at this hour.

Boo's paws were pressed against the front door when I got to it, furiously trying to claw through to the other side. I looked through the peephole and sighed. I'd seen enough of the Luciana family for one day.

"It's almost midnight, Carlo," I said through the door. I yawned. "Can it wait until morning?"

"No. Open the door. And put the gun down."

He spoke with confidence, as if he knew the pistol was aimed right at him. He was right.

It was. I swept Boo off the ground and stepped outside, pulling the door closed behind me. In a lowered voice, I said, "I can't talk to you here. Not right now."

"Why are you whispering?" he asked. "Don't you live alone?"

"Yes, but—"

He raised a brow. "You don't want me in your house. Why?"

"I just have someone—"

Carlo swung his arm around me, thrust the front door open, and stepped inside. "Who's here? Show yourself."

I grappled for his arm and missed. He forged ahead.

"It's not what you think," I said. "If you could just listen to me, I can explain—"

He flicked his wrist, disregarding my words. "Are you seeing someone else? Is that what's been going on the last few months? You're stepping out on my brother?"

"I'd never...let me explain. Outside."

Too late.

Shelby rounded the corner, her hair damp and unbrushed, her body covered in nothing but a polka-dotted push-up bra and panties. "Well, hello to you." She flaunted a seductive grin. He quickly looked away.

"Who's this?" Shelby asked. "Friend of yours? Boyfriend? Is this the guy you ditched my dad for?"

"Her what?" Carlo asked.

I glared at Shelby.

"He's no one." I pushed my hand to Carlo's chest, steering him backward. "He was just leaving. Put some clothes on."

"Why? I'm not naked."

"This isn't the beach. Your attire isn't appropriate for company."

"My *attire isn't appropriate*," she mocked. "You're funny."

Carlo brushed past me—again. "Who's your father, and who are you?"

"Her name is Shelby," I replied, "And she was just going back to bed."

"No, I wasn't," she spat.

I shot a snarky glance in her direction. "Carlo is in the FBI." I paused, allowing the magnitude of his profession to sink in, and then followed up with, "Now go call your father like we agreed and watch *him* for me while I step outside."

I set Lord Berkeley on the floor.

When the horrified look in her eyes abated, she spun around, Boo in hand, and without another word, swayed her butt cheeks from left to right, prancing back to the guest room. I could only imagine what it was like to parent her full-time.

Carlo followed me outside. "Are you going to tell me who her father is? Who *she* is?"

"Who he or she is isn't important right now."

"It is to me."

"It shouldn't be. Why are you here?"

"Tell me who they are, Sloane."

I gripped the door handle. "I'm going to bed. Goodnight."

He placed his hand on my arm, stopping me.

"I want to hire you," he said.

I hadn't seen that coming.

"Hire me? Why? Don't you have your own people?"

"Things are...complicated right now. There's something I can't share with the bureau—not yet."

I took my hand off the knob. "I'm listening."

"I need you to find someone," he said. "I'd arrange it myself, but for reasons I'd rather not discuss right now, I need to focus on my family. Giovanni needs me. Daniela needs me."

"Are you leaving?"

He shook his head. "I'm finding it hard to focus on the bombing and mediate for my family at the same time."

Mediate?

I ran my hands up and down my arms. The chill of night had me wishing I'd snagged my coat from the hook inside the hall closet. Carlo didn't seem to notice or care. Maybe chivalry *was* dead.

"Am I in some kind of trouble?" I asked.

"What do you mean—with whom?"

"Your family. Giovanni seems to think he put Daniela's life in danger, my life in danger, his own life. I need to know what's going on."

Carlo's expression was a mixture of uncertainty and possibilities. He caught me staring, and his face went blank. "I told you. He's not himself right now."

Bed Of Bones

73

"Is anything he said true?"

"You have nothing to fear from my family or anyone affiliated with it. Daniela is safe, and I'm sorting out the rest. Will you help me, or do I need to find someone else?"

I wanted to say no. I deserved to say no. I'd now spoken to all three siblings in the same day and hadn't learned a damned thing.

"Who am I looking for?" I asked.

"A woman."

"Does this woman have a name?"

"Melody. Melody Sinclair."

CHAPTER 12

The name was familiar. I was sure I'd heard it somewhere before.

"Melody produced *Bed of Bones*," Carlo said.

"I remember now. They were talking about her on the news. She's missing?"

He nodded. "No one has seen or heard from her since the explosion."

"Is it possible they just haven't identified all of the bodies yet?"

"Everyone is accounted for now," he said, "except her. I want you to do some digging, but if it turns out someone took her and we've got a murderer out there, I'll take it from there. I won't put you in harm's way."

Harm's way was the only way I'd ever known.

When my body temperature reached shut down, I excused myself for a moment, fetched a blanket from my bed. Shelby's voice trailed through the hall. She was on the phone, talking to her father. Talking and not yelling. I considered it progress.

I sat next to Carlo on a patio chair. "What do I need to know about Melody Sinclair?"

Carlo arched over, relaxing his hands between his knees. "I met Melody many years ago when she was a film student at NYU. I'd stopped by a café one weekend when I was in town. She was refilling some guy's coffee at another table when I first saw her. We locked eyes. I couldn't look away. Her face reddened when I kept staring until finally she winked at me. I don't know how to explain it, but there was an instant bond between us—a connection—like I'd known her all my life." He leaned back. "I must sound like a lunatic."

"You're talking to a woman. It sounds wonderful."

"It was. Over the next month, whenever I was in town, we spent all of our free time together. Even though it was only a handful of weeks, by the end, I knew I wanted to be with her for the rest of my life."

"Why aren't you?"

"My father."

Having never met Giovanni's father, I had imagined what Luciana Senior must be like based on the secretive, yet successful nature of his three children. Thoughts swirled inside me, none of them good.

"So your father found out you were seeing Melody, and—"

"He put a stop to it," he said.

"By doing what?"

"He forbade me to see her."

"Why? Didn't he want you to be happy?"

"He had other plans for me."

I surmised one of those plans included his current position in the FBI.

"I was the brains," he continued. "Giovanni was the firstborn son. The leader. In my family, everyone has a role to play whether they like it or not. It's been that way for generations."

"What about what you want?"

"You don't understand."

I understood perfectly.

"In my family, you do what's expected," he said. "For a brief time, I considered eloping, cutting myself off from the family, but I couldn't. I had to choose. So I did. Did I choose wrong? Probably. It doesn't matter. It's all in the past now."

"Did Melody ever know how you felt about her?"

"She knew, she just didn't understand. I didn't expect her to. She thought we could go to my father, explain things."

"And you've kept in touch?"

"I hadn't heard from her for quite some time. Several years ago she called me unexpectedly. She was single. I was single. We got together. I knew she was still trying to break into the movie industry so I took her to a premiere, introduced her to some influential people, tried to help her out."

"It must have worked."

"Not in the way you think," he said. "She refused my help for the most part. Everything she's accomplished, she did on her own. She was determined to make a name for herself the hard way."

"How did she meet Giovanni?"

"The premiere after party was at his home. I received an important call and had to leave. I asked Giovanni to keep an eye on her for me."

"So they aren't—and they never…"

"No, Sloane. They're just friends."

As if on cue, my body relaxed. "Do you have a timeline for Melody last night?"

He reached into his pocket, handed me a slip of paper. "It's not much, but it's the best I can do right now."

I unfolded it, looking over the notes he jotted down. None of it seemed new or useful, a fact I'm sure he already knew.

"Why weren't you with her?" I asked.

"At the movie premiere?"

I nodded.

"I was supposed to be. I had some family business. It couldn't wait."

It never could.

"Take me through what you know about Melody's whereabouts that night."

"Before the film started she went on stage and introduced the movie," he said. "Giovanni said she seemed happy and calm, excited for the film to debut. After her speech, she was supposed to return to her seat, but she never did.

"How did she exit the stage?"

"There's a passageway on both sides. It's used to shuttle people back and forth without being seen. My brother watched her exit. Minutes later the place blew."

"How much time had passed? Did he say?"

"His best estimate, not more than ten minutes. He assumed she'd gone to the ladies' room, but when the film came on and they dimmed the lights, she still hadn't made it back to her seat. Her assistant said something to him about Melody going to her car, saying she should have returned already. He sensed something was wrong and sent Lucio to find her."

"Is that how Lucio—"

"He stood up the very moment the bombs detonated. A piece of shrapnel severed his jugular vein.

The coroner said he went into some kind of hypovolemic shock and bled out."

"Hypo what?"

"It's when your heart doesn't pump enough blood through your body. Your organs fail, and, well, to put it plainly, you die."

We sat, somber, in silent reverence for the dead. Not just for Lucio, but for all who'd lost their lives. Every second that ticked by ignited my resolve to find out not only what happened to Melody and the others, but why.

"What I am about to say is confidential," he said. "Just between us for now. Understand?"

I nodded.

"Melody is the FBI's prime suspect."

"Why? Just because no one can find her?"

"There's no body, and the building has no surveillance cameras. It's like she walked off the stage last night and disappeared."

"It doesn't prove anything," I said.

"You have to admit, if anyone else came to you with this, you'd suspect her too. I know she's innocent, but until I can prove it, I'd rather my affiliation with her not be brought into the open."

"I understand," I said. "I just have one more question."

"Go on."

"When was the last time you two spoke?"

"A few months ago."

"What was her demeanor like—happy, sad, agitated in some way?"

"Nothing she said gave me cause for concern. She acted normal, happy, herself. My opinion? Whoever bombed that building took her. What I don't know is why."

I intended to find out.

CHAPTER 13

A soft hush lingered in the morning air. I wasn't used to the eerie silence. Not here. Not in a town so jubilant and bright. The festive spirit had been snuffed out, replaced with a feeling of fear, helplessness. The question on everyone's minds: Will it happen again?

The grocery store was deserted except for a handful of people wheeling rickety carts through the aisles. I used the self-checkout, swiped a full-size bag of crunchy Cheetos through the scanner, and paid. Then I walked next door and sat down.

Carlo took a manly gulp of his specialty coffee and leaned in.

"How's Shelby?"

"Sleeping," I said.

"Still not going to tell me who she is?"

I didn't respond.

"All right. You want to tell me why you asked me here?"

"I thought a lot about what you said last night," I said.

"And?"

"I'll find Melody Sinclair on one condition."

"I thought you agreed to it last night."

"I never said I would," I said flatly.

He crossed a shoe over one knee. "I don't care what your fee is, I'll pay it."

"I don't want money. You're Giovanni's brother— I'd never ask."

"You want something, or I wouldn't be here. Am I right?"

"I need answers, Carlo. Whatever is going on with your family, I have a right to know."

"You don't *need* answers, you *want* them. There's a difference."

He ran a hand through his thick, perfectly brushed hair.

"I do something for you, you do something for me," I said. "And don't lead me astray. Give it to me straight. I can handle it."

"You don't understand what you're asking."

"Yes, I do. And if you knew all the assumptions I've made over the last year on my own, you'd tell me just to keep me from poking my head in places you don't want it to be."

He took another swig of coffee.

"Do we have a deal?" I asked.

"Do I have a choice?"

I interpreted this as a yes.

"What's Giovanni's role in the family business? Does he run it? What about you—what's yours? And is there any chance, even a slight one, that Giovanni was the target yesterday? Is any of this somehow related to your family?"

He jerked the chair backward and stood, wrapping a firm grip around my arm. He pulled up, yanking me out of my seat, pulling me close, his coffee-flavored breath filling my ear. "Keep your voice down. Not another word."

A man dressed in a plaid flannel shirt with a long, thick beard glanced in my direction, his eyes focused on the firm grip Carlo had on me. "Unhand the lady."

Carlo spoke through gritted teeth. "Stay out of it."

With his back to the man, Carlo didn't see him rise, but he heard the man's chair as it dragged across the floor, the grating sound like fingernails on a chalkboard.

In a standing position, Plaid Shirt Guy had twice the girth and was a foot taller. He thumbed in Carlo's direction. "Ma'am, is this guy bothering you?"

"I…he's…no. I'm fine. Thank you."

"You sure?"

I glared at Carlo.

He released my arm.

Plaid Shirt Guy looked at Carlo then the door. Carlo got the idea. He walked away, turning before he stepped outside. "Are you coming?"

My heart thumped wildly. I didn't move. I didn't speak. I just stood there. The door slammed shut. I still hadn't moved. Plaid Shirt Guy muttered something. A question. But my focus wasn't on him—my phone was vibrating. I reached over, grabbing it off the table. I had one text message from Carlo in capital letters: DO YOU WANT ANSWERS OR DON'T YOU?

I stepped outside. Droplets of water fell from a tumultuous sky, pelting my face. A black Porsche skidded to a stop beside me. The passenger door opened. Carlo said, "Get in."

A wave of nausea ripped through my body.

Have I crossed the line? Have I pushed too far? What's happening now?

"Where are we going?"

"Sloane, you're trembling and you're soaking wet. Get in the car. There's nothing to fear. You know me."

I knew he was Giovanni's brother. I knew he was FBI. But did I *know* him? Really?

I didn't.

I got in anyway.

CHAPTER 14

"I always wondered if this conversation would come about," Daniela said. "Only I thought you'd be having it with Giovanni and not with me."

The two of us sat next to each other on a sofa in Giovanni's office. Daniela crossed one leg over the other, resting a hand on top of her knee. An emerald ring was looped through a silver chain around her neck. It sparkled like it had just been shined. I hadn't picked up on it the day before at the hospital. I was sure it was just one of many things I'd missed.

"I'm guessing Carlo dropped me off so we could talk, so why am I here?"

She strained a smile, fidgeted with a crystal button that had popped out of the hole on her blouse. "They know who you are, what you do for a living."

" *They*—who? The Mob?"

There it was. I'd said it.

She met my gaze and smiled. "Cosa Nostra. Yes."

Finally. The truth.

"All right, *they* know who I am. So what?"

"Personal relationships—they complicate things."

"In what way? Giovanni has always kept his business dealings from me."

"It's not just a business. It's *everything*. Lately he's been preoccupied—becoming soft. He's not himself."

"You say it like it's a bad thing."

"It can be."

Her voice was flat, monotone.

"From what Carlo told me, you sound a lot like your father."

"I sound like someone who cares about your life," she said.

"Meaning?"

"My family's concerns about you are twofold. You're much more than the average private investigator. The longer you've been with Giovanni, the more questions you ask. You've been digging, looking into our family background."

"How did you—?"

She swished a hand through the air. "It's not important."

"Giovanni was right, wasn't he? I am in danger."

She shook her head. "No one has any wish to harm you. My father is aware there was a time when you saved my life. My mother is dead. I am his only daughter. He's grateful."

"Your brothers refuse to tell me about your family. Why are you?"

She leaned back, folded her arms. "Several months ago Giovanni went to see my father. He wanted out. He felt he'd put in his time over the years, and, if you want my opinion, I believe it happened because he felt you slipping away."

I had no idea.

"How did your father react?" I asked.

"You don't make a deal with the devil and walk away."

She was right. You don't walk. You *run.*

"Are you comparing your own father to the devil?"

She snickered like I'd just made a silly joke. "I love my father, but he isn't the kind of person you trifle with."

"I take it he wasn't keen on Giovanni's request."

"He said no. In fact his exact words were he'd 'have to be dead before I'll allow you to step down.' Giovanni was outraged, as you can imagine. He threatened my father. When he left, my father sent some guys to Park City to find out what had changed, why my brother was acting like a different person. That's when they learned about you. Before then, they had no idea you existed."

The room was cool, but a hot, tingling sensation tore through my body. They'd seen me—they'd seen us—together. They'd followed me. For how long, I didn't know. I didn't want to know. The thought of outsiders spying on me, capturing intimate, private moments of my life took me back to a memory of Sam Reids, the man who murdered my sister—a serial killer, and my stalker. It was a mental place I didn't ever want to go again.

"The men you say came here, was this a few months ago, around the time you disappeared?"

She nodded.

"Giovanni found out they were here, of course, only he didn't know why. When they found the answers they were looking for, they left. And I did too."

"Your father's men took you?"

"Not exactly. I went with them."

"Wait—what? Giovanni said you'd been kidnapped."

The way she smiled while recalling the events surrounding her now "alleged" kidnapping rubbed me in all the wrong ways. It was like she relished it—the attention—the chase. Growing up she may have been a shiny beam in her daddy's eye, but I was willing to bet her brothers were awarded most of the attention. After all, they were daddy's little protégés.

"At first, I suppose I can understand why my brothers thought I'd been taken," she said. "I didn't say goodbye. Giovanni came home, and I was gone."

"Why didn't you say something? Why put him through what you did?"

"I was with my father in New York City, and he didn't want them to know where I'd gone. Not at first. I thought I had time, at least a few days before my brothers came looking for me. But once Giovanni detected I was gone, he began searching." She looked away. "It was stupid of me, I know."

"And when they found you—what then?"

"My father handled it. He said he was just an old man who missed his daughter, wanted her back home. He tried to convince them they worried for nothing. Carlo believed him, but then, he always does. Giovanni didn't. He'd tried several times to get in touch with my father. My father didn't answer. It was unlike him."

"I don't understand. Why all the secrecy? Why couldn't you be honest about why you left?"

"Neither one of them would have sanctioned it, if they knew the real reason I was there."

"Which was?" I asked.

"I volunteered."

"To what—work for your father?"

"In a way. After you left the hospital yesterday, I spoke with Giovanni. I know he thinks the explosion was a personal attack on him, that somehow he's being shown what happens when you try to leave the family. He's wrong. Whoever is behind this cruel, sadistic act, it isn't affiliated with us."

"You told him, right?"

"I...not yet. Carlo brought you here today for a reason." She paused then said, "I'm taking Giovanni's place, Sloane."

Now I understood why I hadn't seen Daniela wearing the necklace before. I understood why Giovanni had a thick, white area on one of his fingers, and why she wore it as a necklace instead of a ring. It was too large to fit on her finger. The signet ring had been his. And she'd decided it was rightfully hers.

"You're taking his place? You can do that? You're a—"

"Woman? Things have changed. My father needs someone he trusts, a person who will get the job done. While I was gone I was being groomed. Tested. My father wanted to be sure I could handle the responsibility."

I couldn't believe what I was hearing.

"Why would you want this life for yourself?" I asked.

"Do you remember the night you rescued me in Salt Lake City after Parker Stanton tried to force himself on me, as he had with so many other women in the past?"

I nodded.

"I wasn't going to his place that night to be with him," she said. "I was going there to kill him. Turned out he was a lot stronger than I gave him credit for, so I ran. But I didn't forget. And even after all this time, his father is still paying people to prove his son's death wasn't a suicide. He thinks somehow, someday, he'll find proof of his son's murder." She leaned forward, curling her bottom lip into a provocative grin. "Do you want to know something? He never will."

In my life, I chased after the truth with such delirious passion, thinking once I found it my mind would finally be at ease. That I could rest easy, satisfied with the knowledge placed before me. In reality, at times that very truth sliced through me like the edge of an executioner's sword, hacking into my soul until, at last, it was extracted from my body and separated from me.

And to think, two years earlier I actually thought the Mafia no longer existed.

CHAPTER 15

Brynn Rowland had a gap between her two front teeth wide enough to slip a penny through the slot and eyes that reminded me of a mood ring. Depending on where I stood, the color was always changing. I guesstimated her age to be somewhere in the almost-thirty range. But one of the things I was known for was my grossly inaccurate perception of age. Her left arm was in a cast. The rest of her body, the parts I could see, appeared like they'd been spared from serious injury.

Even hunched over in the hospital bed, I could tell she was taller than the average woman. Stronger too. So when she squeaked a barely audible "hello," when I entered the room, it caught me off guard.

"How long have you been Melody Sinclair's assistant?" I asked.

She rested her uninjured arm on the blanket in front of her. "Three years."

"What's she like?"

She started to answer, then looked at the television overhead. The screen flaunted a bikini-clad picture of Melody along with the caption:

BOMBING SUSPECT STILL MISSING.
INVESTIGATORS PROCESSING EVIDENCE FROM
SUSPECT'S CAR FOR CLUES.

In the photo, Melody grasped the railing of a boat with both hands, a cruise ship from the looks of it. She stared straight at the camera, her eyes gleaming, full of life. A soft smile stretched across her face. She certainly didn't look like a killer.

Brynn stared at the TV for a few seconds then shifted her gaze to an artificial plant in the corner. A single tear trickled out of the corner of her left eye, sliding down her cheek. She wiped it away. I grabbed the remote, switched the television off.

"Melody is a nice, caring person," she began. "She didn't *do* anything. Not what they're suggesting. She'd never hurt anyone. She couldn't."

"I'm not saying she did."

Brynn blinked away a few more tears. "Then why are you here?"

"Melody has some very powerful friends. One in particular wants to know what happened to her that night and why. I'm here on his behalf. I'm not with the police."

"So…you're trying to find her before they do?"

Nicely put.

For all the "innocent until proven guilty" talk touted by the law, putting Melody on blast across every major media channel in the nation didn't make her the victim, it made her the villain. The public had already decided: guilty. Convincing them otherwise wouldn't be easy.

Brynn reclined back onto the pillow behind her. She fisted a hand, rubbed her eyelid. "I want to help you, but I don't know what happened."

I tried a simpler approach.

"My grandfather once said most of the time the people closest to us hold the key that unravels the mystery. You might have valuable information and not even know it."

"Such as?"

"Let's talk about the night of the movie premiere. When was the last time you saw her?"

"Right after she introduced the film on stage, before the movie started."

"What time did her speech end?" I asked.

"Maybe 11:15 or so. I met her in the hall at the front entrance of the theater."

"What did she say?"

"She'd misplaced her glasses and wanted to see if she'd left them in the car. I offered to go so she wouldn't miss anything. She said no, told me to go inside. I figured she'd run right out and return within a minute or two, so I did what she asked."

"How long after she walked outside did the explosion happen?" I asked.

"Five or six minutes maybe? I heard the movie come on, but I wasn't watching it. I was looking at the theater door, waiting for her to come in. I kept wondering what was keeping her and figured she hadn't found the glasses yet."

Her eyes brimmed with tears, her words jagged, struggling to surface. She swept her uninjured hand beneath her nose, wiping the fluid away.

"Can I get you anything?" I asked.

"No. Thanks."

I reached for a box of tissues on a shelf, plucked a few out, handed them to her. "Take your time."

"It's just...I should have been there, you know?" she stammered. "I should have gone to get those glasses for her, but she insisted."

"It isn't your fault."

She nodded like she'd already been told that a dozen times today. I expect she had.

When her emotions settled, I continued. "You were staring at the door to the theater, waiting for her to come in. Then what happened?"

"I heard a loud "pop," and felt a sharp pain. Blood was all over my shirt. I wasn't sure if it was mine or someone else's. I looked down, and that's when I saw it." She hoisted the blanket, revealing a bandage taped across her abdomen. "A piece of metal sliced through my shirt, pinning it to my skin. It was sticking right out of me. I tried to pull it out. It was too deep. I kept staring at the blood—there was so much blood—and, I must have passed out. When I woke up, I was here."

I winced. She was lucky to be alive.

"Do you remember seeing anyone who looked out of place, anyone who may have seemed suspicious, or shouldn't have been hanging around the theater?"

"I was so busy preparing for the movie to start, it's all a blur. People were coming and going around me all day, but I couldn't tell you what any of them looked like. It's like I saw them but I didn't really *see* them, you know?"

I shifted gears.

"Did Melody have any enemies? Any trouble in her personal life?"

Most of the time when I asked this question, I received a resounding "no," so it was a revelation when she blurted, "She had a stalker."

Bingo.

"When was this?" I asked.

"After we started filming."

"Did she know him? Was he in her life in some way—an ex-boyfriend, maybe?"

"He was a stagehand. Most people didn't pay him any attention because he was quiet, a loner. He never talked much to anyone, and when he did talk, he didn't like looking people in the eye. He bugged me though, even from the beginning."

"Why?"

"His eyes. You couldn't ever see them. His bangs hung past his nose. He wore silver bracelets, long chains over his shirts, and his fingernails were polished a matte grey color. He wasn't thin though. He looked like Severus Snape on steroids."

"How did the stalking begin?" I asked.

"He left flowers in her trailer. There was never a card, so we didn't know it was him at first. Then I caught him following her. We'd be at a restaurant, look out the window, and there he was. We started seeing him all the time. I'd show up at her house and find him parked across the street, staring through her front window like some kind of deranged psychopath."

"What did Melody do?"

"At first she was polite. She thought he had formed some kind of innocent crush. She decided it was best to let him down easy, so she told him she wasn't interested."

"How did he react?" I asked.

"When we arrived on set the next day, he'd taken a two-by-four to some of the props, destroying them. He was fired. When he showed up at her house again a week later, she called the cops, filed a restraining order."

"Did it help?" I asked.

"We didn't *see* him again, but he let us know he was still around."

"How?"

"He left typed notes on her car, in her trailer. Well, not notes, really. More of biblical threats, I guess."

"What do you mean—scriptures?"

She nodded. "From the book of Proverbs."

"Do you remember the exact chapter and verse?" I asked.

She nodded, again. "Proverbs 19:9: A false witness shall not be unpunished, and *he that* speaketh lies shall perish."

"Lies? Did either of you have any idea what he meant?"

"I don't know. She never talked to him. We just figured he was mentally unstable."

If Melody was being looked at as a suspect, every bit of her life was being dissected. They'd know about her stalker.

"Do you know this kid's name?"

"Shane Drexler."

"Is it possible to get a list of the names of everyone who worked on the movie—cast, crew, anyone who came into contact with Melody over the last year?"

"You want to talk to Ronnie Chapman. He's Terry's assistant."

"And Terry is...?"

"The assistant director. You can't talk to him, though."

"Why not?" I asked.

"He's in critical."

"What row was he in?"

"The first one."

"And you?"

"Second. Melody would have been in the second too."

Right next to Giovanni and Lucio.

I handed Brynn my card.

I was almost to the door when I was sure my name was called. I turned. "Did you say something?"

She looked scared, like she was afraid she'd done something wrong.

"There's…umm…one more thing. But if I tell you, are you gonna tell the cops?"

I shrugged. "Depends on whether it's important or not. I can't make any promises."

She mulled it over.

"You know I can't leave here now without you telling me what it is, right?" I said.

"I never planned on keeping quiet, but I didn't expect people to come in here, talking about Melody like they know her. They don't. I was just trying to protect her. I don't want any trouble."

"I understand," I said.

"I have her bag."

"Her purse?"

"Yeah. Maybe something in it will help you find her."

I skimmed the room, expecting it to be in plain sight. It wasn't.

"Where is it?" I asked.

"Not here."

"How did you get it?"

"The day of the premiere, she was preoccupied. She kept leaving her bag everywhere. Finally, I convinced her to hand it over, and I chucked it inside my car. When I went to the hotel to change clothes, I left the car running. I was just going upstairs for a quick change and didn't want to leave her bag on the seat. I took it to my room, but I was in such a hurry, I left it there on accident."

"Where is it now?"

"Ronnie has it."

"Why?"

"We share a room together." She gave me a curious look. "Yes, we're in a relationship if you're wondering."

"Where can I find him?"

She bit her lip. "It's just…Ronnie—"

"Brynn, I appreciate you being honest with me. I need you to trust me. I'll give it to someone who will get it into the right hands and not the wrong ones. Okay?"

I exited, my pace slowing as I noticed the bald men who had so vigilantly kept watch outside Giovanni's room were gone. I peered inside. The room was empty.

"Can I help you, Miss?"

I spun around, facing the young, blond nurse behind me. "The man in this room. Did you move him?"

She blushed. Giovanni had that effect on women.

"He left," she said matter-of-factly. "Mr. Luciana checked himself out yesterday. Had an older man with him claiming to be his family doctor."

"The man—did you see him? Do you know what he looked like?"

"Well...I remember thinking he seemed a bit old to still be a doctor. But who am I to say?"

"What age would you say the older man was?"

"If I was guessing, maybe eighty or so."

"Anything else?"

"He walked with a cane. Black, if I remember right. It had a silver handle."

"Did they say where they were going?"

"Not to me. My superior said he'd be looked after at his own home."

She pivoted and walked away.

I sagged against the wall, catching my breath. I'd been with Daniela only two hours before. Giovanni wasn't there and I hadn't heard from him. I wondered...had Carlo or Daniela? Was I the only one left in the dark?

CHAPTER 16

Ronnie unbolted the door to his fancy hotel room, cracked it open, and poked his head into the hallway, looking both ways before waving me in. Although it was evening, the sun had finally dodged the clouds long enough to brighten up the remainder of the day. Ronnie's curtains, however, were drawn.

In a pair of khaki slacks and a tucked-in, blue-and-white striped Polo shirt, Ronnie easily had ten or more years on Brynn. His heavily hair-sprayed, brown hair looked like someone had placed a bowl on his head and cut all the way around the edges. Every strand was perfectly placed, making me wonder if it was actually a cheap rug he'd purchased from the five-and-dime. I resisted the urge to tug on it and find out.

"Is…everything okay?" I asked.

He leaned against the counter, tried to appear debonair.

"Why wouldn't it be?"

"Are you nervous?"

He shoved his hands in his pockets. "I'm fine."

"You're shaking."

"No, I'm not."

I suppose watching his arms spasm right in front of me was an optical illusion. The heater kicked off with a bang. A startled Ronnie shot into the air.

I dismissed it, sat at the table, crossed one leg over the other. "You seem a little on edge. Want to tell me what's going on?"

His nostrils expanded. "Nothing."

"What row were you sitting in when the film started?"

"You're here for a purse. Why do you want to know?"

"What row?" I repeated.

"The first. Right next to Terry."

Interesting.

"I don't see any injuries," I said. "The people sitting in the first couple rows suffered the worst, and yet you don't have a scratch on you. Why?"

He walked over to the bed and bent down, hoisting a blue leather handbag off the ground. It had fringed tassels on both sides and a white skull on the front. I liked it.

"Here," he said, dangling the bag in front of me. "Take it."

What he meant to say was: take it and go.

The bag slipped off his fingers, plopping down on the table.

He folded his arms and waited, his forehead creasing when I didn't rise.

"You got what you came for; you can go now," he insisted.

"You didn't answer my question."

"Maybe I don't want to."

I leaned back in the chair. It was firm and uncomfortable against my bony posterior, but I wanted him to think I was relaxed enough to stay all day. "Maybe I don't want to leave."

He made a huffing sound.

I smiled.

"Are you always so pushy?"

"When I need to be—yes," I stated.

He sat down. "I was hungry. I hadn't eaten all day."

I hoped the conversation about his food cravings would lead somewhere productive.

"*Okaaayyy.*"

"I saw a couple lights on inside a fast food joint across the street, so I walked over. I figured I had enough time to place an order and get back in time for the movie. When I got there, the doors were closed, locked."

"Why are you telling me this?" I asked.

"You asked why I don't have any injuries."

"Were you in the theater when the bombs went off or weren't you?"

"I don't feel comfortable talking about this—I don't even know who you are."

I leaned forward, extended my hand. "Sloane Monroe. I'm a private investigator. Now, did you see something?"

He scratched behind his ear.

He had.

"Ronnie. Look at me. What...did...you...see?"

"Nothing!"

"You're lying," I said.

A phone jingled nearby. His body quivered. He looked like he wanted to crawl under the table and hide.

"Are you going to answer it?" I asked.

"What?"

"The phone."

"It can wait. I'm sure it's nothing."

He pressed his hands together, briskly rubbing them back and forth like he was trying to start a fire without any matches.

"Let me ask you something," I said. "When the theater exploded, did you race back to check on your boss, your friends, your girlfriend, anyone? Or did you run?"

He attempted to suck air into his lungs with a series of rapid, shallow breaths. His face reddened. He grasped his throat with his hand, pointed with the other. "My…inhaler."

"Where is it?"

"Suitcase. Side pocket."

I unzipped the top of the case, retrieved the inhaler, and pressed it into his hands. The phone was ringing again. While he administered a few pumps into his lungs, I followed the sound. It was coming from the bathroom. By the time I stepped inside and found the cell phone, the noise had stopped. Again.

Ronnie's footsteps rapidly approached. I flung the door shut, locking myself inside. He pounded and wailed against the door like a child, begging me not to touch what didn't belong to me. But I'd already seen what he was so afraid of. There were numerous incoming text messages—all the same—all from the Bible. All from the book of Proverbs. But it was a different verse this time, 1:16: For their feet run to evil, and they make haste to shed blood.

I opened the bathroom door, my gun aimed, ready. "You better start talking."

CHAPTER 17

The presence of a pistol directed at the center of Ronnie's head made him sing like an actor on Broadway.

He confessed, saying before the blast he'd witnessed two people standing close to one another outside the theater. They appeared to be engaged in a conversation of some kind. From his vantage point, he was unsure whether they were male or female. One was larger in stature. Based on this, Ronnie concluded he was a man. He wore a heavy coat and a tight, dark cover over his head. The other person looked more like a woman. Her body was blocked by the man, but at one point Ronnie saw her hand, dainty and petite, too small to be male.

When the theater exploded, only one thought had pierced Ronnie's mind: getting inside and finding his friends. He sprinted back across the street. As he entered the parking lot, a man slapped closed the door to a fossil of a pickup truck. Ronnie had cupped his hands around his mouth, shouting "hey" in the man's direction. The man turned. Ronnie recognized him. It was the same man he'd seen in the parking lot not a minute before. A ski mask was half on, half off his face, like he was in the process of removing it when he'd been interrupted. Upon seeing Ronnie, the man fisted his hands, his boots crunching through the snow, making a beeline straight for him.

Ronnie didn't know why, but his instincts told him to flee. Fast. In the process, his cell phone slipped from his sweat-drenched hands, plummeting into the snow.

He didn't stop.

He didn't look back.

He just kept on running.

Ronnie had made it to the hotel, his insides still empty, legs weak. He hunched over, leaning an arm against the prickly stucco exterior of the hotel. He gulped big pockets of air and closed his eyes, summoning the courage to glance behind him. He did so slowly, while at the same time reaching inside his pocket for the key card he needed to slide through the metal slot in order to gain entrance to the hotel. A family of four had exited a silver minivan, the children asleep in their parents' arms. He saw no one else.

He'd swiped his card and tried not to focus on the throbbing pain shooting through his legs as he ascended two floors to his room. Safely inside, he collapsed onto the desk chair, grappling for the landline phone next to him. He'd planned to call the police, tell them everything. Then Melody's phone buzzed, and he saw her purse. The phone was inside it, and he dug it out, stunned when he noticed the number on the caller ID.

It was his.

Someone had picked up his phone.

What he didn't know was why they were using it to call Melody.

He'd tossed the phone on the bed, confused. The caller hung up and redialed, again and again. The phone went silent for a time and a text message popped up. A photo of Brynn. Her face had been crossed out, a thick, red X slashed with a marker. Under her name was a scripture: Proverbs 1:16. Ronnie had slammed the curtains shut, fiddled inside the drawer next to the bed, found the Bible. He read the passage, contemplated its meaning. His only thought had been that if he told anyone what he saw, then Brynn would be a dead woman.

"These scripture references," I said. "They mean something."

"Yeah, they mean the guy is twisted, screwed up in the head."

As much as I wanted to continue the back-and-forth banter we were sharing, Ronnie needed to share his story with the investigators working on the case. In the meantime, I decided to squeeze what I could out of him before I forked him over. He seemed suspicious of this and refused to answer any more questions, saying he wouldn't put Brynn's life in danger.

"If you sit me in front of a bunch of nosy detectives, I'll lie," he said. "I'll tell them I didn't see anything." Then he glared at me, his arms folded tight in front of him, a non-verbal display that he was closed for business.

Too bad for him; I was wide open.

In his frenzied rant, he'd missed all the obvious holes required to plug the questions that would arise when he plead the Fifth, like explaining why there were multiple calls placed from his cell phone right after the explosion went off to the one person investigators wanted to find most, and why a scripture message had been sent with Brynn's photo attached.

I pulled out my phone and sent a text. Ronnie's brow furrowed. I smoothed it out by requesting a glass of water, saying once I drank it, I would leave. I had an ulterior motive, of course. He got the water and I sipped it, slow and steady, like if I drank it any faster, my mouth might burn.

I smiled. Ronnie relaxed. He thought he was about to get what he wanted: my departure, posthaste.

Then Carlo arrived.

...

Carlo didn't acknowledge Ronnie when he entered the hotel room. He didn't even glance in his direction. He placed his gloved hand out, palm up. I inserted Melody's phone into his palm. He dusted it, then scanned it, searching through her text messages, her recent calls, her emails.

Ronnie remained at the table, enraged. He thought I'd tricked him. I suppose I had. For a split second, my thoughts turned to Giovanni. I wanted to know where he was, how he was doing. If anyone had answers, Carlo did. But we were here for another reason.

Carlo looked at me. "According to these text messages, Melody received a similar scripture message every hour on the hour the day her film premiered."

"I know," I said. "While I was waiting for you to get here, I ran the number on her phone log. It's a prepaid cell phone."

"A burner. Thought so."

"If he purchased it with a credit card, the company he bought it from would have destroyed the transaction record. And if he didn't use a card, odds are he purchased it with anonymous digital crypto currency."

"Bitcoins," he said. "He could have avoided using a financial institution to pay for the phone and transferred the money directly from a computer. Either way we're screwed." Carlo shifted his gaze to Ronnie. "How did he know Melody's phone was in your possession?"

Ronnie studied his hands, kept quiet.

"Is this how it's going to be?" Carlo prodded. "I'm giving you a chance, one chance to tell me what you know."

Again, nothing.

Carlo opened the door, letting in one of the bald men I saw keeping watch outside Giovanni's room at the hospital. Baldie's arms were crossed in front of him, showcasing his bulging biceps. He approached Ronnie, his enormous hand swooping down, smacking Ronnie on the side of the head. Ronnie didn't move, he didn't blink. The same couldn't be said for his perfectly-placed toupee which shot across the room like a hairy torpedo. Ronnie bowed his head, flattened both hands on top of the stringy locks that remained.

Baldie smacked him a second time—harder. Then again—harder still. After the third hand lashing, I heard a crack. A gash, the length of a dime, seeped blood from the side of Ronnie's head. Baldie watched it drip before glancing down at his own ring finger, eyeing the thick metal like he was more concerned that the piece of jewelry was all right than Ronnie. Wouldn't want to upset the wife, I guess.

Before the fourth blow, the force of which I expected would either send Ronnie flying or put him into a coma, I wedged myself between Baldie's hand and Ronnie's head. I shielded my arms over my face, braced for impact. Baldie stopped midair.

I looked at Carlo. "What is this? There are better ways to question him."

"Until he cooperates, I'll do what I need to do."

"So you're going to what—beat answers out of him?"

"I *will* have the truth before I turn him over," Carlo replied. "All of it. Stay out of the way, Sloane. This is how we do things."

I didn't care. It wasn't how *I* did things.

I glared at Baldie, my hand outstretched, finger wagging toward the door. " *You*. Get out!"

Baldie looked at Carlo like I had some kind of nerve. I did. I had all kinds. In the past I'd sanctioned unorthodox measures when the moment called for it, but not here, not like this.

"Give me a minute with him," I said. "Just one."

Carlo ran a couple fingers across his chin, considering my plea. He wasn't smiling. He grimaced, looked at a forlorn Ronnie who'd rounded his body into a ball. Carlo held up a single finger. "One."

One tilt of Carlo's head and Baldie lowered his hand and started for the door, his shoulder colliding with mine as he passed. He grinned. I didn't care. I got my one minute.

After they stepped into the hall, Ronnie looked up, opened his mouth.

"Don't," I said. I crossed the room, wet a washcloth in the sink, handed it to him. "Shut up and listen. If you value your life, you *will* answer all of his questions."

"I thought you said he was a cop? That other guy, he's no cop."

"It doesn't matter what they are or who they are. You might not believe this, but keeping valuable information to yourself isn't helping anyone. If you think this is bad, wait until they get you into the interrogation room. You know what federal agents call a person with nothing to say?"

He shrugged.

"Guilty," I said.

"I'm not."

"I believe you, they won't," I said. "And neither will your friends, your family, your parents. How would you like Mom and Dad to see your face plastered all over the five o'clock news?"

He shrugged.

I braced my hands on the sides of his chair, leaned in. "Do you want to help Brynn or don't you?"

"I *am* helping her. If I say something...she...that maniac will get to her. He'll kill her."

"If you don't, Carlo will kill *you*."

I had no way of knowing how far Carlo would really go, but at this point, I was ready to say anything.

Carlo reentered the room, alone, right on cue. He glared at Ronnie. "I'll ask you once more: How did he know the phone was in your possession?"

"If I tell you, what will you do to protect Brynn?"

At the mention of her name, Carlo glanced at me, holding my gaze for a few seconds before turning his attention back to Ronnie. "You have no right to ask anything of me when you've offered nothing in return."

"I don't care."

"Do you value your life, Ronnie?"

"I value hers."

Carlo ran a hand across his brow. "Fine. I'll make sure someone is stationed outside her room."

"When?"

Carlo closed his eyes, his patience waning. "As soon as you answer my questions."

Ronnie looked at me. I nodded.

"The photo of Brynn that he sent me—it wasn't a photo I had in my phone," Ronnie stuttered. "I recognize the top of her dress. She was wearing it the night before the film premiere at a gala honoring all the films being shown during the festival."

"Where was this?"

"In a conference room at the Hotel Tremonte."

"So he's been watching you—all of you. Taking pictures. Why?"

"I don't know," Ronnie said.

"Brynn suggested the biblical threats came from Melody's stalker," I said. "Maybe he followed her here."

Carlo crossed his arms in front of him. "We know about Shane Drexler. He was picked up at his residence in California earlier today. He worked the night shift at a fast food joint every day for the last week. From what we can tell, he's never even stepped foot in Utah."

Ronnie piped up. "Maybe he has an accomplice, someone on the outside. It could happen, right?"

"It's possible, but stalkers don't usually work in pairs," I said. "This guy could be some low-level acquaintance she crossed paths with long before she hired him. He noticed her, she didn't notice him."

I looked at Ronnie. "You saw him—the bomber—that night."

"It was dark."

"Still, you must have picked up on something," Carlo said. "There are a few overhead lights in the parking lot. How tall would you say he was?"

"About your height."

"Build?"

"He was wearing a coat. He looked big, bulky, just like everyone else."

"Was there anything on the coat he wore or any of his clothing—a logo, a brand of any kind?"

Ronnie shrugged. "Like I said, it was dark."

"Was any of his skin exposed?"

"Almost everything was covered up. He had a mask over the top half of his face. Stopped right under his nose. I think he might have been taking it off when I interrupted him."

"Anything else?"

Ronnie pointed at me. "Talk to *her*. She knows everything."

Carlo plucked a phone from his breast pocket and sent a text. We stood around for a couple minutes, sweat forming on Ronnie's forehead as he considered what might come next. Two men entered, their federal agent cards dangling from the breast pocket of their dark, uncomfortable-looking suits.

"What's going on?" Ronnie asked.

"I've asked Federal Agents Grant and Lourdes to escort you to the station so they can take your statement," Carlo said coolly. "I expect you to tell them the truth and answer any questions they have. Understand?"

Ronnie wheezed, reached for his inhaler. I rescued the toupee from the ground, ran my fingers through it and straightened the pieces as best I could. I tried not to focus on the amount of particles and germs I was touching. I'd never actually held fake hair in my hand before. It was surprisingly soft. Who knew?

"The safest and best thing we can do for you is get you out of here," I said, handing over his hair. "Trust me. The police station is a good place for you to be right now."

He returned his focus to Carlo. "And Brynn, she'll be protected, right?"

Carlo smiled, patting Ronnie on the shoulder. The agents accompanied him outside.

When everyone had gone, I said, "He did what you asked. Make the call. I want to keep this girl safe."

"There's something we need to talk about first."

"If this is about your sister, yes, we talked. And no, I can't have this conversation right now. Your family drama will have to wait until—"

"Sloane, Brynn Rowland is…"

He looked away.

"Is...what?"

"Gone."

"What do you mean, Carlo?"

Without looking back at me, he said, "She's been taken."

CHAPTER 18

"What do you mean—*taken?!*" I demanded.

"She was abducted from the hospital a short time ago."

"But...I was just there."

"I'm aware. The team is going over the surveillance footage now."

"You knew all this time, and yet you led Ronnie to believe you could protect her. I don't care about your passion to find Melody Sinclair. It's wrong, Carlo. Ronnie trusted me. He deserves to know the truth."

"And he will."

"When?"

"As soon as they're done making sure there's nothing else he's hiding. Until then, there's no reason to agitate the man more than he already is at present."

I wanted to walk out, leave him standing there, and I almost did, until he offered to give me the details about Brynn's abduction.

The hospital surveillance footage, he explained, showed a severely drugged Brynn being wheeled out of the hospital, her head slumped to one side. For a minute she looked like she was about to collapse. The person pushing her, clad in light-blue medical scrubs, held her shoulder as he sauntered his way through two hallways and down the elevator like he had every right to be there. And it had worked.

The man managed to keep his head down, shielding his face from several predictably-placed cameras. Investigators hoped they'd find something, anything they could use. For all the advancements in technology, I wondered why no one used wall cameras. I'm talking the moveable kind, ones with the ability to record a person from all different angles, like the kind used in the sea of reality television.

Carlo said the man had made it outside with Brynn in tow without so much as a second glance from the hospital staff. A surgical mask covered his face, providing the perfect shield to protect his identity, just as the ski mask had done before. He had dark hair, brown from the looks of it. Whether it was real or not or how long or short it was had yet to be determined. Outside cameras showed Brynn being rolled to the edge of the parking lot where he picked her up out of the wheelchair, cradling her in his arms, before he walked through a patch of trees, fading into the night.

CHAPTER 19

Shelby tapped the tips of her fingers on the counter, her unpolished nails looking like they'd been gnawed down to the bone. She groaned like she was in physical pain. "How long are you gonna keep me cooped up in this house?"

I pulled a barstool out, sat next to her. "You know I can't take you with me while I'm working. It's too dangerous."

"Yeah, yeah, I get it. You have more important things to do."

"Shelby, there's a lot more to life than your teenage drama with your boyfriend. I'm trying to save lives."

She slurped a few sips of soda, then chucked the empty can across the kitchen. The can tinged against the outside of the garbage container, then fell to the ground, splashing brown liquid all over the tile floor. She didn't get up. Upon hearing of the spill in aisle one, Lord Berkeley trotted over, licked a few drops of soda from the floor, and then pushed the can around with his nose. I hopped off the stool, discarded the can, toweled up the mess.

"You can go home whenever you like." I nodded toward her phone on the counter. "Call your father right now."

She snickered, but didn't reach for the phone. "It's late. I'll wake him up. Maybe tomorrow."

"Do you really think he'd care about the time? He'd be in his truck and on the road in less than five minutes."

"Yeah, I guess."

"Look," I said, "I know what you told me the other night about the fight you had with your father, and maybe that's a small part of it, but I don't need to be the mother of a teenager to understand there's more to it. It's hard for me to believe this little act of defiance is only over a boy."

She looked like she wanted to cry. I expect she needed to.

"Do you see your mom often?" she asked.

I couldn't tell whether she was trying to change the subject or bond with me.

"My mom passed a long time ago," I said.

"Oh."

"Why do you ask—have you heard from your mom recently?"

"Nope. Don't care to either. She walked out on us, and as far as I'm concerned, she can keep on walkin'."

Over the last two years, she'd been abandoned by her mother and watched her grandfather pass away. The strain, the acting out, made more sense to me now.

"I've never met your mother," I said, "but I was grateful to have known your grandfather before he died."

"I'm just so tired, ya know?" Her voice was shaky.

"Why don't you get some rest? We can talk more in the morning."

"Can I ask you something?"

"Sure."

"How do you get over it?" she asked.

"Someone dying?"

She nodded.

"You don't. I don't think we're supposed to. Your grandfather would want you to keep him in your heart, but he would also want you to move on with your life. He'd want you to make good choices. Focus on what you have, not what you don't. Look around. Your father, your grandmother. They're still here, and they love you."

"I know."

I now saw something else in her—shame.

"I lost my sister to a serial killer several years back," I said. "For a long time, it consumed me. I felt everything—pain, regret, hate, revenge. I felt crippled. I couldn't move on. It wasn't until I learned to let go and to focus on what I have instead of what I lost that I started to get myself back again. We get what we give in life. Find what inspires you, what motivates you to get out of bed each day. Even if it's one thing at first. Learn to appreciate the small things in life."

In the middle of my "boost your confidence" speech, Shelby split open my bag of Cheetos, crunching her way through a quarter of the bag. Maybe I was wasting my time.

"I knew my grandfather was sick. He told me. But I guess I never thought he'd die. Not really. He was more than a grandfather, he was my friend. I told him everything. And now my dad…"

My heart raced. "What about your dad? Is something wrong?"

"He's all right. It's just, I worry. He's all I've got."

Without warning, she sprung from the chair, wrapping her slender, noodly arms around me. At first, I stiffened. I hadn't recalled ever being embraced by a teenager before. Hugging had never been a strong point with my parents when I was growing up. Neither had compliments or positive reinforcement or the encouragement I needed to believe in myself. I'd learned all of those things from my own grandfather.

So many years between us, and yet, here we were, sharing a common bond. I raised my arms from my sides and did the one thing that didn't feel natural: I hugged her back.

CHAPTER 20

The chamomile tea wasn't doing its job. Not even a little bit. I'd downed one cup, then two, and was currently three quarters of the way through my third. My anxiety hadn't quelled, my mind still unsettled. No word from Giovanni. No word from Melody.

Where was he? Where was she? And where was Brynn?

In full "I feel like a failure" mode, I grabbed the remote, flicked on the television, and clicked through channels like a restless insomniac. It was a little after three in the morning. Soon it would be four, and I'd still be awake. Wrestling.

I dipped my pinkie finger inside a plastic bottle, raised a small, yellow, oval pill from the bottom, and swallowed it.

Xanax.

It wasn't like I wanted to take it.

I didn't *ever* want to take it.

I needed to. And that was the hardest thing to admit of all. I always waited, thinking my mind would clear eventually. Sometimes it did. Other times it just kept spinning, faster and faster like a glass plate on top of a pointy stick.

I suppose that's what made me a good private investigator. My mind, in its random and sporadic state, had the ability to process several different scenarios at the same time, all with unique, yet plausible outcomes. The scenarios were like doors. The tricky part was deciding which was the right one to walk through, and which was the wrong one. Pick the right door, find the answers I sought. Pick the wrong door, risk a life. Maybe even multiple lives. It was this harsh reality that paralyzed me more than anything.

I leaned back on my pillow, closed my eyes. I saw Melody. I saw Brynn. I saw the scriptures, the words running over and over. Melody's stalker hadn't sent those messages like everyone had assumed, and perhaps he hadn't sent the flowers. There had been someone else on set. But for how long? And why? And why Melody?

I thought about the bombs. They were amateurish in nature, and though they hurt many and in fact killed a few, it could have been much worse. It was almost like the bomber had controlled the chaos to some extent...why?

There was more to it, something I wasn't seeing.

Maybe the demise of all the people in the theater wasn't the big motive behind the blast. I asked myself: What else had been accomplished by this bomb?

The film had shut down, possibly for good.

I needed to see that movie.

CHAPTER 21

Morning blew in the bitterest chill of the year and a low, dense fog clinging to the air like a veil that couldn't be lifted. Two hours earlier, Shelby had finally succumbed to sleep after trying to make it all the way through a slasher marathon on TV. At least she was sleeping. She needed it. Then again, so did I.

I scooped Lord Berkeley into my arms, grabbed the phone off the nightstand, and wrapped an afghan around myself. Then I stepped outside and dialed Cade.

"I was just about to call you," he said. "How is she?"

"Fine. She thinks she runs the place."

He laughed.

"Are they any closer to findin' out who's responsible for the theater bombin'?"

I filled him in on what meager details I had.

"Sounds like you've got your hands full. I'll come get her."

"If you want the truth, I think she's ready. We had a nice talk last night. I won't say I was able to impart a lot of female wisdom, but something got through."

"She say much about the trailer trash she's been hangin' around with lately?"

"A little. She was more interested in talking about your father. If you want my opinion, what she's really after right now is your attention. She's getting it from this Jace guy, but I think she'd rather get it from you."

He sighed. "There are better ways to let me know."

"And maybe when she's thirty she'll grasp that concept. Right now, she doesn't know any different."

"What do you suggest?"

I never thought I'd be the one giving advice.

"Your father's death has made her think a lot more about everyone in her life. She worries about you."

"Me? Why?"

"Think about it. Your wife walked out, your father passed away. She's scared, Cade."

"I'm not goin' anywhere."

"I know."

"Can I talk to her now for a minute?"

"She's asleep, but I can wake her."

"No, don't. I've got a meetin' at noon with Chief Rollins and some of the other guys about a case we're workin' then I'll head your way."

"Call me before you get here. I'll come home."

"Will do. And Sloane…thank you."

CHAPTER 22

Giovanni sat beside me in the car, his hands interlaced together, resting on the knee of his light grey tailored suit. We'd just finished having breakfast at a diner where neither of us talked. I mistakenly thought food would help soothe my nerves. It hadn't. I felt worse. If it would have been dinner, I would have called it the last supper, because that's exactly what it felt like.

"I'm leaving," he said.

Outside, snow began to fall.

"I know. You told me the other day. Is that why you wanted to see me again?"

He nodded.

"Okay."

He reached over, rubbed my arm. "Don't do this," he said.

"Do what?"

"Act like everything is fine. It isn't. You don't have to be tough, Sloane. Not around me."

I sat back, rested my trembling hands in my lap. "I haven't heard from you in two days. *Two days*, Giovanni. I thought you were already gone."

"I'm here now."

"Yeah…to say goodbye."

The last word—*goodbye*—hadn't rolled off my tongue as easily as I hoped it would. If he detected a change in my tone of voice, it didn't show. I gazed out the window. I wanted to forget where I was, what was happening. The flakes of snow were bigger now, blowing across the front of the car like cotton spinning inside of a giant machine.

"Lucio's funeral is tomorrow," he said.

"In New York?"

He nodded.

"I'm sorry. I'm going to miss him."

He squeezed my arm. "Me too."

"How's Daniela?"

He frowned.

"I spoke to her—"

"I know," he said.

"Then you know what we talked about?"

He was rubbing my arm again. "I'm sorry."

Sorry. That was new.

"I should have told you," he continued. "It should have come from me—not my sister. You had a right to know."

"So why didn't you?"

He sighed. "Before we met, I didn't think about the way I was living. It's easy not to when it's all you know."

"And after?"

"I wanted a different life."

"I thought you were getting out. If you are, why do you have to leave—why can't you stay here?"

"Is that what my sister told you—I was getting out?"

Either he was still in charge of the family, or Daniela had lied.

"Daniela seems to think she has everything under control."

"She doesn't," he said.

"What do you mean?"

He hesitated.

"Even now, after everything I know, after coming here to say goodbye, you're not going to tell me?"

He took a long, drawn-out breath. "My father never planned on making my sister head of the family. This whole thing, the entire plan, was a ploy to get me back where he thought I needed to be."

"I don't understand. She told me your father tested her. He was confident she could handle the responsibility."

"No. He used her to get to me. He knew I'd never allow it."

"You'd sacrifice the opportunity to change your life in order to save hers?"

What was I saying? Of course he would.

"For her, I would do anything. You'd do the same if it was your sister."

I had done the same.

"I want to stay," he said softly. "I want to be here—with you."

I could feel myself starting to crack, at that pivotal moment when the egg breaks and the liquid inside comes dripping out.

When I didn't respond, he said, "What would you have me do?"

I wanted to get out of the car—my car—and run. "I would have you do exactly what you're doing, but it doesn't mean I…that I don't…I want you to…"

"If you ever need me, for anything—"

"I know," I whispered. "You'll always be here."

Only he wouldn't. I bit my lip, tried to silence my emotions. It was too late. He reached out, reeled me in, held me close. I could hear his heart pounding through his chest. I didn't want to move. I didn't want to ever move. I was sobbing now, creating a big, clear stain on his silk, button-up shirt. His fingers trailed through my hair, soothing me. I didn't feel any better. I felt cold and hollow. Vulnerable and ashamed. And like so many times before, I felt alone. Sooner or later, no matter what they promised, all the men in my life had walked away.

He bent down, his hot breath steaming my eyelids as he spoke. "I love you, cara mia."

The door opened, and he stepped out. I wiped the tears from my face and looked up. He didn't turn back like he often did. I imagined it was too hard. I hoped that on the inside, he was crying too. He closed the car door. And in the drifting snow, I sat and watched the only man I'd ever truly loved walk away.

CHAPTER 23

The Sundance Film Festival offices were inside of a two-story log building that looked more like the cabin a family lived in than a place of business. Had it not of been for the eight-foot-long canvas banners draped along the outside, displaying a variety of this year's films, I would have driven by, thinking I was at the wrong location.

I reapplied makeup to my tear-stained face, took several cleansing breaths, and entered. A blond-haired, blue-eyed kid sat behind a log desk. I say 'kid' because anyone ten years or more my junior appeared that way to me lately. He had Hugh Grant hair and wore white shorts, some fancy tennis shoes with bright yellow shoelaces, and a hoodie that said Park City across the front. His legs were hairless like he shaved them every day. They looked cold. He reached into a bag of tortilla chips, pulled a handful out, swirled them inside a bowl of orangish-colored queso, and then plopped them into his mouth, crunching down with an expression on his face like he'd just had a bite of better-than-sex cake.

After the blissful moment passed, he noticed me standing in front of him. He quickly wiped his hands, staining the front of his shorts in the process. He interlaced his fingers behind his head and leaned back in the chair as far as it would go. He flicked his chin up and said, "Hey," like he'd just taken voice lessons from Joey Tribbiani.

"Hey," I replied.

"What can I…uhh…do for you?"

He smiled, wide. I imagined he'd *do* just about anything I wanted.

"Is there any way I could screen one of the films from this year?"

"Tell me which one and I'll give you the schedule."

"So, are all of the movies up and running again?"

"Yep. Most of 'em anyway. They just started back up today. Not a very big crowd, though."

I leaned forward, lowered my voice. "I was actually wondering what I'd need to do to get a private screening?"

He squinted like he didn't understand. "Everything is public. You just have to go and see the movie."

"I'm willing to pay."

"Oh, well, you don't actually buy the tickets here. The ticket office is—"

He wasn't getting it.

"I meant I'd be willing to pay extra for the chance to see a certain film alone."

I had no intention of paying the "extra" myself, but one phone call to Carlo was all it would take. Besides, he'd lied to Ronnie. He owed me.

"Well, see, it doesn't work like that."

I waited, wondering if the pilot light inside would ignite.

It didn't.

Never a quitter, I had decided to try again when a plump woman in a full-length sweater dress rounded the corner. She looked to be in her sixties and had pulled her salt-and-pepper hair back into a too-tight bun that made her look like she should be living in Asia. She arced her head when she saw me, her cat-shaped glasses sliding an inch down her nose.

"What's going on here?" she asked.

"This lady is trying to see one of the films by herself," the kid said. "And I was just telling her it doesn't work like that."

Idiot.

"She even said she'd pay 'extra' to see it by herself. Funny, huh?"

Double idiot.

"A hoot." Her nose wrinkled in more ways than I conceived possible. "Who are you and what are you really doing here—are you press, police, what?"

I paused, considering my next move. I didn't have one.

"Well?" she demanded.

I extended my hand. "Sloane Monroe."

She didn't accept it.

"Yes, but what are you doing here, Miss Monroe?"

"I wondered when you'll be showing *Bed of Bones* again?"

"We won't. It's off the agenda for now. Sorry."

"But you have copies, right?"

"Digital, yes. Why?"

"I'd like to see it."

"There are plenty of other films playing this week. Buy a ticket."

"I don't want to see anything else."

"Well, you haven't much choice," she huffed.

The kid's eyes lit up, finally. *Ding, ding.* Only he'd identified what I wanted a little too late. He moved behind the woman and signaled me with his right hand, pointing at a side door on the other end of the building.

I looked at the woman. "Sorry I bothered you." I returned to my car. I watched. I waited. No kid. Maybe I misunderstood whatever he had tried to tell me. It was still early, and already it had been a rough day.

I started the car. A hand reached out from the side of the building, waving me over. I drove around.

"Who are you?" the kid said, approaching my open car window.

I had nothing to lose.

"I've been hired to look into what happened at the theater."

"So you *are* a cop then?"

"It doesn't matter. Can you help me?"

"I can't get you a copy of the movie."

Then there was nothing more to say. I put the car in reverse, prepared to back away.

"Hold on…hold on," he said. "I know someone who can tell you everything you need to know about the movie."

"Who?"

"My grandfather," the kid said, beaming with pride.

"Your grandfather? What does he know?"

"Everything. My family settled this place. They erect it."

"You mean erected?"

He pointed, giggling under his breath. "Yeah, what you said."

"What does that have to do with the movie?"

He leaned in. "It was my grandfather who told the director all about this place. You can find him at the museum. He runs it."

CHAPTER 24

My cell phone buzzed. Caller unknown. I put the phone to my ear and listened.

Breathing. Slow and heavy. Raspy, like he'd spent his life with his mouth wrapped around a cancer stick.

Somewhere, somehow, he'd tracked me down.

I jerked the car to the side of the road and slammed it into park. The breathing was annoying. I wanted it to stop.

"Who are you?" I asked.

"I lead in the way of righteousness," he hissed.

His voice was stronger, much more sophisticated than I imagined.

"There's nothing righteous about killing innocent people."

Asshole.

"Don't blaspheme."

"Against who—you? How about don't kill? You read the Bible, you understand the Ten Commandments, don't you?"

"Stop."

"Or do you only read from the book of Proverbs?"

"Don't," he demanded, louder.

"A false witness shall not be unpunished, and *he that* speaketh lies shall perish. Recognize it?"

"Stop it!"

"How about this one. 'For their feet run to evil, and make haste to shed blood.'"

Silence. Good. At least the breathing had stopped.

"What do they mean?" I prodded. "What are you trying to prove?"

He growled like he wanted to reach through the phone and strangle me.

"*Where* is Melody Sinclair? *Where* is Brynn Rowland?"

"Soon. Very soon."

"What's soon?" I asked.

"Don't get in the way."

"Too late."

Silence.

"You called me. Obviously you want something. What is it?"

The line went dead.

I locked myself inside the car. I slouched down in the seat. I popped open my center console, unzipped my binocular case. I looked around. Then I made a call.

"Carlo, I—"

"Sloane, are you okay?"

"He contacted me."

"Giovanni, I know. I just spoke with him. I don't know what to—"

"No—the man who took Melody, and Brynn, and who knows who else."

"And Victoria Broderick."

"Who?" I asked.

"She's an actress."

"Why her? What's the connection?"

"She played the wife in *Bed of Bones*."

The wife of whom? I wondered.

"How is she missing? I thought everyone was being detained."

"We don't have the resources to hold every single person. Best we can do is keep the ones who can give us the most information. We cut everyone else loose yesterday. They were supposed to be on the buddy system, not go anywhere alone. He still got to her."

Thanks for keeping me in the loop.

"Three women in three days, all familiar with one another, all related to the movie. It means something."

"Yeah, they're looking into the connection."

"It's the movie, Carlo."

Obviously.

"We know. We're dissecting every second of it."

"How did you know Victoria Broderick was missing?" I asked.

"One of her friends was supposed to pick her up at the hotel, take her to the airport. She got there, and Victoria was gone."

"Did you find anything—a cell phone, anything with some sort of scripture reference?"

"Several partials in her room. But it's a hotel. Could be from anyone."

I informed Carlo about the conversation I'd just had with our killer. After I finished, he said, "It's time I bring you in on this, officially. Let me handle getting everyone up to speed on how you're connected."

"Fine. Fair warning, expect fireworks when everyone finds out I've been involved all this time."

"Where are you?"

"Old Town," I said. "Across from Sampson Law Office."

This was true. The museum was across the street. If he wondered what I was doing there, he didn't ask.

"Give me twenty minutes, then come in."

"Can it wait? There's someone I need to talk to first."

"I need you here."

"It's important, Carlo."

"Fine. Make it fast. I want the address of the place you're going."

I gave it to him.

"You've got to assume he's out there," he warned, "watching your every move."

For me, it was just another day on the job.

CHAPTER 25

In all the years I'd lived in Park City, I was ashamed to admit that not once had I visited the museum. I'd thought about taking a tour on several occasions. I'd even sent in a generous donation during last year's fundraiser for a bigger, better building. I always knew one day I'd make it here. I just didn't know it would be on a day like today.

The man I was looking for was named Walter Thornton. I found him inside an office, his nose stuck in a book, an Egyptian travel guide from the looks of it. He wore a blue cardigan sweater over a pair of wool slacks that looked like they were thick enough to repel snow. His head was angled down, allowing me to see the ample hair atop his head, proof that not all men had hair loss at his age.

"Planning a trip?" I asked.

He looked up. His wrinkly, crooked smile made me think of my grandfather. "Pardon?"

"The guide you're reading," I pointed. "Is it any good?"

He tipped it up, allowing me a visual of a pyramid on the front cover. "Quite good, yes. I'm planning a trip next year. Have you ever been?"

I shook my head.

He removed his reading glasses, pinched the rim while rubbing an eye. He may have been tired in body, but he was robust in spirit. "I expect you're not here to discuss the marvels of Egypt, although I'd be happy to, if you like."

Straight to the point—a quality I admired in a man.

He stuck out a hand, displaying the thickest fingernails I'd ever seen. "Name's Walter. But my friends call me Butch."

I took his hand in mine. His grip was firm, like a single squeeze could cause permanent damage. "Good to meet you, Walter."

"Butch."

"I understand you worked with Melody Sinclair on the movie *Bed of Bones*."

He placed a cloth bookmark inside the page he was browsing and closed the book, setting it flat on a shelf behind him. "I wouldn't say we worked together, but she did consult with me on a few things the way one consults with a forensics expert on a television program, I suppose."

"What did you two talk about?"

"I provided her with information on some of the town's history, answered a few questions, tried to make sure she had her facts straight."

"And did she?"

He narrowed his eyes. "I can't say. I haven't seen it yet. She emailed me an attachment a few months ago. Couldn't get the file to open on my computer. A message kept popping up saying something about the file being too large to download."

If his computer was even a fraction as old as he was, I could see why. Still, I was surprised he hadn't asked his ever-so-adept grandson for help.

"I wanted to wait and see it on the big screen, and I had tickets too," he continued. "Miss Sinclair mailed them to me. I planned on taking my wife. Then, well, you know what happened." He stared at me for a moment. "I'm sorry...I didn't get your name, young lady."

I gave it to him.

"What is it you do, Miss Monroe?"

"Find people, mostly."

"People like Melody Sinclair?"

The man didn't miss much.

"Are you aware she's missing?" I asked.

"I watch the news. Shame what happened to the old cinema building, to all the poor souls inside. Glad most of them made it out alive. Hard to believe Miss Sinclair's a suspect though."

"Why?"

"I won't say I'm an excellent judge of character, but she doesn't strike me as the type who'd harm anyone."

"Can you tell me what *Bed of Bones* was about?" I asked.

"The old silver mines." He pressed a thick, yellow fingernail onto the top of the desk. "This place, this town right here, used to be one of the biggest money-makers in America. You familiar with the history at all?"

"Not really."

"How much do you want to know?"

"Everything," I said.

"You ever taken a tour of this place? I'd be glad to show you around."

"I'd love to, but not today. Right now I need to know about the movie. If you help me out, I promise I'll return when I can and take you up on your offer."

He angled a crooked finger toward a chair. "You're after the dark history then. Best sit down. You might be here awhile."

I sat, wondering how dark such an exuberant place could be.

"Tragic story, really," he began. "It all started in the fifties when two boys wandered off their grandfather's farm. The boys' father, Harvey, had brought the family out as a kind of vacation while he negotiated the sale of his father's place."

"Where was Harvey's father?"

"He'd passed away. Cancer, as I recall. Anyhow, the oldest boy, Willie, was a teenager at the time. Curious, just like any other kid his age, I expect. Just looking for a little adventure. Decided to take his younger brother, Leonard, along for a walk around the place. It was a bad idea, which Willie didn't realize at the time. The land surrounding the family farm was littered with mines, which was exactly why their mother had warned them not to go beyond the gate surrounding the property."

"What threat did the mines pose to the children?" I asked. "They were no longer in use, right? Weren't they abandoned by that time?"

He raised a brow. "So you do know a little history?"

"Some."

I felt like the star student in class.

"The mines may have been deserted, but giant holes still remained in the ground."

"Why weren't they sealed?" I asked.

"It wasn't a priority. After the stock market crashed in 1929, the mines never fully recovered. Don't get me wrong, several attempts were made to get things running again. They spent years trying to revitalize what once had been a booming, lucrative industry, but eventually the town's population dwindled to around a thousand or so, and the mines shut down for good."

"You spoke of a tragedy. Did something happen to the boys?"

He cleared his throat. Not a good sign.

"Willie and Leonard discovered an open mine shaft, and, from Willie's account of things, all Willie wanted to do was look at it. A toy Leonard was carrying fell into the opening, and, being as young and innocent as he was, he must have thought he could reach in and get it."

I clasped a hand over my chest. "What do you mean—*reach in*?"

My stomach churned.

"Some of the mines were deep," he said, "almost one thousand feet beneath the surface. Poor Leonard fell to his death."

I clasped a hand over my mouth. The accidental death of an adult was painful enough. The demise of an innocent child stirred an entirely different kind of emotion. "Was his body ever recovered?"

"It was a huge undertaking, but Harvey was adamant. He wasn't about to leave his boy down there. He wanted Leonard to have a proper burial alongside his own father."

"It must have been devastating to lose a child in such a way," I said.

"Willie suffered the most. I saw him once in town about a month after it happened. The two of us were about the same age at the time. He was with his parents. I knew it was him because he was the only one in town I hadn't seen before, and the rumor about what happened had gone around."

"I'm sure he blamed himself for what happened."

"They all did, seemed like. Willie's parents walked around like a couple of living corpses, like they'd lost the will to live. It was too hard for them to stay here. They took the property off the market and left town."

"Is there anyone in the family still alive?" I asked.

"I'm not sure. I never saw Willie again. Leonard was their only other child. There's little chance the parents would still be alive today."

Was the story of a young boy falling down a mine shaft compelling?

Yes.

A tear-jerker?

Yes.

A full-length movie?

I didn't see it unless Melody embellished some of the details.

"I can see why Melody Sinclair was intrigued with the story," I said, "but in my opinion, it would be a stretch to turn it into a full-length feature."

"Based on the boy alone, you're right. The death of Leonard is only the beginning."

"I don't follow."

His chair creaked as he leaned forward, staring into my eyes. "*Bed of Bones* isn't about the death of the young boy, you see. Not really."

I was more confused than ever. "What is it about?"

"Leonard's body wasn't all rescuers found when they reached the bottom of the mine. They found something else, a sight so grisly, so disturbing, even now it's hard to believe it happened here."

"What else was down there?" I asked.

"Dead bodies. Lots of them."

CHAPTER 26

"More dead bodies?" My throat felt scratchy, dry, like it had been raked over with a fork. "How many?"

"Seven," Butch replied.

"Miners?"

"Women, all buried next to each other in a circular pattern, legs straight, arms crossed in front of their chests."

"Like a ritual of some kind?"

"Looked like it."

I thought of the scripture verses, thought maybe this could have been ritualistic in nature. "If the mines were no longer being used, how long had the bodies been down there?"

"That particular shaft hadn't been active for several years. When the bodies were discovered, all they found was skeletal remains. The ligaments and tendons had decayed, leaving several piles of bones buried in the mine bed. This suggested they'd been down there long enough for the bones to rot."

"How do you know so much?" I asked.

He winked. "It's my job to know the history of this town, Miss Monroe. Both the good and the bad. It's a rarity to come across something I don't know."

He said this with pride.

"What can you tell me about the way they died?" I asked.

"It was assumed the women were alive when they entered the mine shaft."

"How do you know? Were they able to determine cause of death?"

"All of them had a single bullet wound to the head, shot at close range with a Colt SAA .45."

"Couldn't they have been shot above ground?"

"Five out of seven shell casings were found in close proximity to the bodies."

"Are you saying the killer lined them up next to each other and shot them, firing-squad style?" I asked.

"A few of the women were matched through dental records. This enabled investigators to create a timeline on how the murders evolved based on the dates the identified women went missing. Some disappeared months apart from each other. Detective Hurtwick, a man in his early thirties, was the lead investigator at the time. It was his first big case. He believed the killer shot and killed his victims within a few days of their abductions. The forensic examiner concurred with this logic. To suggest otherwise meant the killer would have had to keep them alive for months at a time while he perfected his group of seven."

"The women…did they have anything in common—age, hair color, profession?" I asked. "Did they know one another?"

"No. They were as different and varied as a group of women could be. That's what made it so confusing."

"You said bones were found."

"Like they were on display, yes. Although, in my opinion the killer didn't seem to think the remains would ever be unearthed. I believe he returned to the scene of the crime, time and time again, treating the place like his own private cemetery, maybe even thinking he'd created a holy sanctuary of some kind."

"Why would anyone think it was a holy sanctuary?" I asked.

"Behind each victim was a post, a cross made out of pieces of wood."

"Grave markers? Was anything written on them?"

"They all had words carved into the wood."

"Words like the women's names?"

He shook his head. "Sins."

Sins.

"Did they happen to be scriptural references?"

I couldn't imagine anyone, no matter how crazy, taking the time to carve out an entire passage. He shifted in his chair. I had touched on something.

"Most of them were one to three words long: proud, lying tongue, shedder of blood, wicked, mischievous, false witness, soweth discord."

"Seven sins for seven ladies," I said. "Why seven? Why stop there?"

I said this knowing once the vast majority of serial killers had the taste of death in their mouths, it was almost impossible to get it out. Most increased their kills, both in number and frequency; they didn't lessen them. To stop all together took a discipline few possessed.

He turned, extended a hand to a shelf and grabbed a worn, brown, faded copy of the Bible. He opened it to chapter six of Proverbs and handed it to me. "Read verses sixteen through nineteen aloud please."

My heart raced. With a great deal of reluctance, I accepted the book, reading its contents aloud. "These six things doth the Lord hate: yea, seven *are* an abomination unto to him: A proud look, a lying tongue, and hands that shed innocent blood. An heart that deviseth wicked imaginations, feet that be swift in running to mischief, a false witness that speaketh lies, and he that soweth discord among brethren."

Somewhere in the middle of reading, my hands began to perspire. I thought of the scripture the killer sent to Melody. It fit perfectly with a false witness speaking lies. I thought of Brynn. Hands that shed innocent blood. And as for the actress, Victoria Broderick, she could have easily been any of the rest. What had they done to deserve the sentence they were about to receive? Now I had something far greater than a multitude of abductions to fear. I feared the women's imminent deaths.

The sacred book slipped from my hands, thumping on the ground like I'd dropped a sack of flour. I leaned down, picked it up. "I'm sorry…I'm so sorry. I didn't mean to—"

He smiled. "It's all right. Tell me, what has you so frightened?"

"I…it's nothing. I'm grateful to you. You've helped in ways you don't even realize, but I need to go."

He caught my arm with his leathery hand as I rose. "The verses you just read. They mean something to you don't they?"

They meant I had to tell Carlo there was a good chance Melody was already dead.

"Please," he continued, "let me help."

I paused, sat back down. I'd give him two more minutes. Two minutes and I was gone. "I think what

happened to the women all those years ago—the
murders—they're happening again. Maybe even in the
same way they happened before."

"Why do you think this?"

Butch was a wealth of information, a man who, it
seemed, was passionate enough about what he did for a
living to have spent a great deal of his life studying it,
keeping it safe, protecting its secrets. Could I trust him?

While I pondered the question, my hands fidgeted,
unable to keep still, no matter how tightly I clasped them
together. I wondered if he sensed my apprehension.

He said, "Would it help if I told you I understand
why this is happening again and explained why I feel
this way?"

I nodded, hardly believing he was capable of such
a thing.

He continued. "And would it help if I provided you
with the name of the killer?"

His name? Was he joking?

I squeezed my eyes shut, nodded, and braced for
impact.

CHAPTER 27

"Chester Compton."

The name didn't ring a single bell.

"Who is Chester Compton?" I asked.

He paused, building up to the final reveal. "Willie and Leonard's grandfather."

I absorbed his words.

Let them sink in.

"You said Chester Compton was already dead. The family was in town to sell his property. So how did they know he committed the murders?"

"After the women were found, investigators initially focused on the other mines, thinking they might find additional bodies in them too. Every mother, father, aunt, uncle, and brother who'd lost a female of any kind over the past several years came forward."

"It gave them hope," I said. "They thought if the other women turned up, their relatives would too."

"Exactly."

"And?"

"After several weeks of searching, no other bodies were found. In hopes of finding the killer, a statement was released citing the gun cops believed was used in the murders. And Detective Hurtwick received an interesting phone call."

I'd leaned so far forward on the seat, I almost fell off. "From whom?"

"Harvey Compton."

"Willie's father?"

He nodded. "He said while they were packing up his dad's place, preparing for the sale, they found the gun stashed in between the mattress. Hurtwick talked to several gun shops in Salt Lake City and verified Chester Compton purchased the gun some ten years earlier. They got a search warrant and scrubbed the place from top to bottom."

"Did they find anything else?"

"Several typed pages kept in a notebook, a journal of sorts. Read like a personal belief system. It was filled with random thoughts about the women he stalked. He took his time. He knew where they worked, where they lived, their daily routines. The journal spoke of punishing them for their wickedness. The way he talked about them—he didn't see them as humans, he saw them as sinners."

I'd read about this type of person before. Chester Compton was what was known as a missionary type of killer, just not in the biblical sense, although he'd probably convinced himself some higher power led him to do what he did. Missionaries were compelled to kill, on a mission to rid the world of a certain type of person. They saw their victims as worthy of death in one way or another based on the victim's odious actions in life. To the killer these people were undesirable, unworthy to continue on with their lives. Orchestrating their deaths was a favor to the rest of humankind. Death was often impersonal and quick. To the killer, the victim was hated. The Axeman of New Orleans and Caroll Edward Cole both came to mind.

"Did they find anything other than the gun and these pages?" I asked.

"Fabric from the last victim's dress. It had torn off on a nail in Chester's shed. They found the manufacturer, matched it up. The parents confirmed their daughter was wearing the dress the day she went missing."

A message popped up on my phone from Carlo? WHERE ARE YOU? I SAID TWENTY MINUTES, NOT SIXTY.

I was too engrossed in the conversation with Butch to respond.

"Aside from the murders, what type of person was Chester Compton?" I asked.

"He was a prominent member of the community. He threw elaborate parties at his home when the silver mines were booming. He was well liked. My grandparents attended his home on multiple occasions. Neither of them ever suspected a thing."

"Did he live alone?"

"Had a wife. Pearl. She went a little nutty after he died. Didn't want to leave the house for anything. Talked aloud to Chester like he was still there. Even said he talked back to her on occasion. People were concerned, started talking, and her son put her in a home. She died there a few years later."

Chester Compton was dead, and yet, three women had gone missing over the last three days. Someone had renewed his cause again. If anyone could help me, Butch could.

"Three women have gone missing in the last few days," I said. "All three were part of the movie in some way—one a director, one an actress, one an assistant. Two of the three were sent scripture references that tie in to the chapter you just showed me, and I suspect the third received one too—police just haven't found it yet."

"What scripture references were sent to the women?"

I told him.

"Mm."

"What are you thinking?" I asked.

"Those verses are an exact match to the ones sent to two of the seven women discovered in the mine shaft. Vera Robinson and Anne Farmer. Their families found the verses on typed slips of paper. Vera's was found in her car, and Anne's was inside a locker she'd rented at the town pool." He rested his hands on the desk. "Remember before, when I said I could tell you why this is happening again?"

I nodded.

"I put a display together with a few items pertaining to the murders. It wasn't anything large or significant in any way, just a simple glass enclosure about the size of a coffee table. It had newspaper clippings and various other things inside."

"Was there anything of significance?" I asked.

"I'd managed to procure a few of the typed pages some years ago. I made it the centerpiece of the display. I wanted the gun, but they wouldn't release it from evidence."

"Can I see the pages?"

He shook his head.

"Why not?" I asked.

"About eighteen months ago, before we moved into the new building, the display was stolen. I arrived one morning to find the glass case had been shattered with a rock which the thief left behind. Everything in the case was gone. And the strange thing is, far more valuable items in the museum were left untouched."

"Someone came in with the specific goal of stealing the contents relating to the murders," I said.

"I never could prove it, but I was suspicious of a female employee who'd locked up the night before. Always thought she had something to do with it."

"What made you consider her?"

"Aside from the rock, there was nothing to suggest someone physically broke into the place, not through a door or a window."

He watched me glance around the room.

"The old building didn't have surveillance. This one does. As you can see, I learned my lesson."

"Wasn't she questioned?" I asked.

"By a Detective Cooper, yes."

I rolled my eyes.

"You find him as engaging as I do, I see."

Engaging. Never a word I'd use for Coop. Crude, insensitive, and brash, but never engaging. I appreciated Butch's sarcasm nonetheless.

"Did Detective Cooper know you thought she did it?" I asked.

"He was aware of my suspicions, and she was questioned, but there was no evidence to support my argument."

"Where is she now? Does she still work here?"

"I may not have been able to get her convicted of the crime, but I was able to coax her into quitting of her own free will." A look of satisfaction settled on his face. "A few write-ups, followed by a demotion, did the trick."

"Can you give me her name?" I asked.

"Karin Ackerman."

I jotted it down in my head, shelved it for later.

"Why would anyone, after all these years, want to take up the cause again?"

He shrugged. "Why does one do anything? We are unpredictable creatures, all of us. I will say this…I've given it a lot of thought over the years, and I believe it would be near impossible to get the ladies down the shaft alone."

"You think he had an accomplice?" I asked.

"I do. I think someone helped him get those bodies down the shaft."

It made sense. An accomplice would require complete trust, someone who shared in his beliefs. Not an easy combination to find.

"What about his wife?"

"It's possible, although I've seen her in photographs. I don't think she could have managed the weight of anything more than a newborn baby."

"He could have done all the heavy lifting," I said.

"Even if he did, and even if Pearl had helped him, they're both long gone now." He flung his arms in the air. "It doesn't matter how many years have passed, I've always wondered if I was right. Guess I'll never know."

"You said Chester killed his victims over several months. He wasn't in a hurry."

"Probably wanted to make sure he got it right."

This time it was different. These women were taken within a matter of days. They all shared a common bond—the movie. It gave me the sense someone was trying to complete the ritual fast, get it over with. Maybe this person had watched the women for months—years even—waiting for the festival to begin, the perfect time to strike.

"Can you show me the mine?" I asked.

He stood and turned, opening a drawer behind him. "Sure, I have a map of all the mines in the area."

"Not on paper," I said. "I want to go to the exact location the women were found."

"Even if we did, the mine is sealed now. They've all been sealed for years for safety reasons. The only thing I could show you is a mountain of snow. You'd never even know anything happened there."

"I still want to go. I need to see it for myself."

"You can't. Not on foot. We'd need snow machines to get out there this time of year."

There had to be a way.

And then it came to me.

"What are you doing right now?" I asked.

He gave me a look like he knew what was coming. "Why?"

"I have an idea. And Butch…I'm going to need you to send me the attachment of the movie—the one you couldn't open."

CHAPTER 28

It took a lot of convincing to lure Carlo away from the station, but he trusted me enough to follow up on a good lead when I promised one, and once I backed it up with a brief explanation of my conversation with Butch, he decided it was worth his time The three of us met at a small air strip in Heber, where we chartered a private helicopter owned by the Luciana family. Probably owned by Giovanni himself.

While the chopper was being fueled, Carlo pulled me to the side. "I had to do a lot more than twist a few arms to be here."

His eye twitched like he was having second thoughts. I could have soothed him, come up with some witty female comment to make him feel a lot better about putting his job on the line if anyone found out what we were doing, but I didn't. I played the honesty card.

"I can't guarantee what we'll see out there."

"Then why are we here, Sloane? I don't have time for anymore false leads."

"As opposed to having time for what? You don't have to be here."

"Don't get all worked up. I have a right to ask a question."

And I had the right to refuse an answer.

The pilot signaled to Carlo. We were ready to go.

I placed my hands on my hips and stood, waiting. "Are we doing this or aren't we? If you don't believe in me, shut it down. Shut it down right now. I'll find a way out there without you."

He gave me a look like he could stronghold me into the car, haul me off to the station if he wanted.

I'd like to see him try.

Sensing the tension between us, Butch backed away until his shoulder collided against a chain-link fence behind him. He stared at the air strip, pretending like he wasn't privy to our conversation.

For a minute I thought it was a bust. Carlo was hard to read. Even harder than Giovanni. The pilot waved again, like maybe he thought Carlo hadn't seen him wave the first time. Carlo gave him a look: *flail your arms again and I'll sever them from your body.* The pilot put his arms down.

"Let's do this and be done," Carlo said through gritted teeth. He walked toward the chopper, leaving me standing there. When he realized I wasn't by his side, he looked over his shoulder, but kept walking. "Now, Sloane. Now."

I had paused not just because Carlo doubted me…I doubted myself. What if he was right? What *were* we doing? A gentle nod from Butch propelled me forward. Even over a blanket of snow, I had to see the original crime scene.

Once we were in the air, no one spoke at first. Butch sat on one side, Carlo and I sat on the other. Butch was quiet and observant, seemingly pleased to be along for the ride. It felt peaceful floating on air, seeing the clouds dot the skyline. Then my phone rang. Shelby.

There were no pleasantries, no hello, nothing to suggest we'd bonded the night before. Back to square one.

"I got bored, I'm sorry," she began. "Don't be mad, but can I get a ride back to your place?"

"Shelby, I asked you not to go anywhere. I was very clear. Didn't you talk to your dad? You know he's coming today."

"I know, but I got tired of sitting there."

"Where are you?"

"Well…umm…"

"Shelby, I don't have time for this right now. Tell me where you are or you can find your own way back to the house."

I didn't mean it, but under the watchful eye of Carlo, I didn't know what else to say.

"I'm at the police station."

"You're where?" I asked.

"I got busted tryin' to get a ride into town."

"By who?"

"I dunno. Some old guy. I called him Officer Grandpa. He didn't like it. Now I'm here."

She yawned as if it was nothing.

"You expect me to believe he hauled you in just for hitching?" I asked.

"I kind of had my skirt pulled up at the time. Not a lot, just a little bit, I swear. You couldn't see my panties or nothin'. The cop gave me some lecture about what could happen to me, and I mouthed off. Then he shoved me into the back seat of his car and cuffed me. He cuffed me, Sloane. Can you believe it?"

There was one thing I did believe—I wasn't cut out to raise a teenager.

"Does the officer who arrested you know you're talking to me right now?" I asked.

"Doubt it. He passed me off to some other guy who says he knows you. I think he's your friend."

"What friend?"

"Your friend."

"Chief Sheppard?"

I wanted to groan aloud.

"No, your other one. His badge says Cooper."

"Coop?" I asked.

"Yeah, him."

Double groan.

"I told him I was staying with you."

"And?"

"He just laughed."

"Can I talk to him?"

"He's standin' next to me, but, ahh, he's still laughin'."

"Just put him on please."

The phone was passed off. A wheezy guffaw streamed through the air. I tolerated it for several seconds, and when he still couldn't bring himself to talk to me after I'd said hello a handful of times, I practically broke the glass on my cell phone with my finger to end the call. I dialed Cade. Whatever insults Coop had planned for me, they could wait.

"Your kid is going to send me to an early grave," I said. "If she was a child, I'd advise you to spank her until her ass drew blood, and I'm not even a supporter of physical what-you-call-it. Not when it's a kid. She may, however, be the one exception."

It sounded like he was laughing too, but he managed to get out, "What did she do now?"

"Tried to hitch a ride into town, got picked up by an officer."

"Maybe we could convince him to hold her for a while."

We?

"I'm kinda in the middle of something," I said. "How long until you get here?"

"An hour at the most."

"Call the station, let them know who you are, and tell them you're on your way. I'll meet up with you as soon as I can."

Carlo shook his head, indicating his displeasure. At least he didn't say anything.

While I'd been on the phone, Butch directed the pilot to our destination. We were almost there.

"What we're looking for is going to be right through those trees," Butch said.

I peered through the glass, seeing nothing but magnificent pines and miles of white.

"Don't know what you're expecting to find," Butch continued. "I don't even think we'll be able to—"

He stopped mid-sentence.

"What is it?" I asked.

His face paled, the fleshy color turning a somber shade of ash.

I placed a hand on his shoulder, tried to look past him. "Butch?"

It was like he couldn't hear me.

I looked out my window. I saw nothing. Carlo dashed from his seat, crossed to the other side, trying to glimpse what had caused Butch to clam up. Carlo hovered over Butch, his head pressed against the glass. "No, it can't be. Melody."

"Carlo—what's going on? What do you see?"

He turned, gripping the vinyl seat to keep his balance. "Sloane, they're dead. They're all dead."

CHAPTER 29

The killer may not have been able to descend the opening of the shaft given the iron-sealed door and the mountain of snow piled on top of it, but he'd still found a way to carry out the ritual with his own unique flavor. Melody Sinclair, Brynn Rowland, and Victoria Broderick had been laid on top of a section of plowed snow. It looked like it had all been done by hand, hours of work slaving away in the intense cold to make sure it was just right. Then replowing with each snowfall.

The killer had begun to form a circular pattern with the women's frozen corpses. Feet near the center of the circle, the bodies were about two feet apart, arms crossed over chests, heads tilted upward, facing the sky. The bodies reminded me of points on a star. I imagined the killer standing in the center circle formed by the women's feet, pivoting as he cast his eyes downward, observing them one by one.

Crosses fashioned out of what looked like two-by-four pieces of lumber had been staked to the ground about one foot behind each of the bodies. I reached into my bag, extracted a pair of binoculars, zoomed in, focusing on the words on the grave markers. They weren't carved or etched into the wood, they were written, with a thick marker of some kind. Melody Sinclair's cross displayed the words LYING TONGUE. On Brynn Rowland's: SHEDDER OF BLOOD. What blood had she shed? I angled the lenses, searching for the words behind Victoria Broderick's body. Since I had never seen her before, I could only assume it was her. On her cross it said: FALSE WITNESS.

Carlo held out a hand. I inserted the binoculars onto his palm, keeping my hand on them at first. "Maybe you shouldn't," I said. "Maybe you should wait."

"I'll see her sooner or later, Sloane."

He stared through the lenses, his face tight, fist balled up like he wanted to strike. I didn't blame him. Butch's arms were crossed in front of him, his head down, body rocking. He chanted something under his breath, trying to self-soothe.

Carlo made eye contact with the pilot. "Get us out of here. Now."

We'd interrupted the killer's process, stumbled upon his dump site. He was only halfway through the kill process. How would it change things once he found out the ground he considered sacred had been tainted, his precious bodies extracted from the scene?

What would he do now?

Where would he go?

The pilot whisked us away. Carlo frantically made one phone call after another—one to the chief, another to his fellow agents, informing them of our macabre discovery. Once we touched down, Butch and I would be expected at the station, briefed on what we knew, grilled just like everyone else. And the latest crime scene would be yet another one I'd be shut out from.

I glanced at Carlo. His jaw was locked, face petrified, like carved stone. Melody was dead. I wondered if he blamed me in some way for not finding her sooner. I didn't know whether to offer him some kind of comfort or to keep my mouth shut. I imagined neither would matter. It wouldn't give him the solace he needed. It wouldn't bring her back.

CHAPTER 30

I sat through an uncomfortable debriefing at the station, during which Carlo admitted his relationship with Melody Sinclair to the class of investigators, agents, higher-ranking officers, and the chief who'd come up with a name for the guy they were looking for: The Sundance Killer. It lacked creativity, but caught on fast.

No longer a suspect, Carlo behaved like he had no reason to withhold his past any longer. His hiring me, in his words, was "totally justifiable and not to be questioned." I sat beside him, hands in my lap, quiet. Not having anything to say wasn't my usual MO, but the daggers I received from my fellow classmates pierced my soul. And I simply didn't have the will to take them all on at once.

In the middle of what felt like an interrogation process, a kid the chief referred to as Kenny came in with information on the tracks found at the scene. He was tall, lanky, preferring eye-glasses to contact lenses. His hair was short but stuck out like he'd tossed and turned in bed the night before, not bothering to brush his tangled locks this morning. He probably didn't have a girlfriend and didn't assume anyone would care. And with that kind of attitude, he wouldn't have a female companion anytime soon either.

The grin on Kenny's face changed from a confident smile to a look of awkwardness as he approached his waiting audience. I attributed it to the multitude of stressed-out stares coming at him from every direction across the police round table.

At least they'd stopped looking at me.

"Well," the chief flicked a couple fingers in the air, "get on with it."

Kenny coughed and a sound erupted like the last trickle of water filtering down the drain in a bathtub. "Tire manufacturers make several different lines in their tires, all with their own tread design, each in various sizes."

I thought I detected a bit of a speech impediment in his tone, a possible lisp he'd corrected over the years.

"Tell us something we don't know," Carlo added. "This isn't our first day at Police Academy."

Under his breath, Coop said, "Oh, I don't know—it might be for Sloane."

Coop refrained from further comment when Carlo began to rise. The chief leaned over, whispered something to Coop then looked at Carlo like he'd taken care of it. Carlo sat back down.

As the meeting continued, photos sporadically filtered in from the crime scene where investigators were racing to process as much as they could before dark. Judging by the size and shape of the tracks, the women had most likely been transported to the place of their death on a snowmobile of some kind. Whether they were still alive at the time was anyone's guess at this point. Visible tracks led to and from the crime scene, coming to a snow-packed road. It was a road less traveled making it easy to spot tracks made by an SUV or a pick-up truck. This is where the new information came in. Kenny said three-dimensional impressions had been taken and then cast using Plaster of Paris. Given we didn't have a suspect vehicle, I hoped we were all about to get lucky, at least matching the model of tire from the tread pattern.

"When analyzing the tracks, we found the tires were different," Kenny said. "The one on the left didn't have the same pattern as the one on the right. Both had a low amount of tread remaining on the tire. We ran the tracks through the TreadMate database and matched one of the two tires. I have the manufacturer as well as the model if you want to see it." He held a sheet of paper out, glancing around the room like he wasn't sure who he should give it to.

Carlo and the chief both held up a finger at the same time. Kenny walked over, put the paper into the chief's hand. The chief glanced at it then passed it to Carlo.

"Give us a minute, all right?" the chief said to Kenny.

Kenny folded his arms, leaned against the wall behind him.

"I'll need you to leave the room, Kenny," the chief said.

Kenny's face reddened. He bowed his head and walked out.

The chief glanced around. "We done here with this one for now?" He thumbed in my direction.

"For now," Coop said.

"I wasn't talking to you," the chief scolded. He looked at a federal agent opposite him. The agent exchanged looks with Carlo and then gave a slight nod.

My immediate departure was followed by the chief's, who offered my second lecture of the day. I prayed there wouldn't be a third. I hadn't told him I was working with Carlo, something he would view as inconsiderate on my part. Frankly, I was astonished he believed I was going to sit this one out.

His first mistake.

Telling me they had it handled and didn't need my help was his second.

I'd never heeded his warnings before.

The use of the word "ass" shot out of his mouth several times and in a multitude of ways—maybe more times than I'd ever heard it used by a person in one sitting before. For the grand finale, I was given strict instructions not to leave my house without "checking in" first. All of this was said in what I liked to call his "I think I'm being really quiet" voice. Too bad he failed to notice the corn circling around the outside of his office like vultures desperate for a meaty bite.

Carlo dispersed the lurkers and walked in. The chief muttered something about getting me out of there before anything else happened. I walked out. Carlo followed. No matter where I went, I couldn't get a moment's peace.

"Carlo, I'm—"

He took my hand in his. His voice was solid and smooth, but his eyes mourned Melody. "Don't, Sloane. It's not your fault. You didn't kill her. I've been at this job long enough to know what happens when you bear the weight of burdens that aren't really your own. Besides, if it wasn't for you, we'd still be looking."

Such sophistication.

Such kindness.

I didn't deserve it.

"I'm going to have someone drive you home," he said.

"There's no need—I'm fine."

"You're not, and I wasn't asking. I'm working on getting eyes on you while we find this guy. If you leave the house, I want to know."

Excellent. Now two people I needed to check in with. In a single day, the adult had become the child.

Slumped over a metal table in the waiting room was Ronnie, his toupee not-so-firmly back in place. He'd been kept on ice, awaiting the bad news about Brynn. Coop stood over him. Not exactly the kind of person I'd want next to me when I needed support. He placed a hand on Ronnie's shoulder, said something to him. Ronnie wiped his watery eyes, looked up, pointed at me like he knew I was passing by at that exact moment. "Liar!"

It was one simple word, but it spewed from his mouth like the roar of a lion.

His girlfriend was gone, and he blamed me. I tried convincing myself it was only because he needed to take it out on someone, but I never let myself off so easy.

Yet another of my epic failures.

...

Carlo's hands gripped my arms, shaking me. "Hey—can you hear me?"

Someone said something. A female. I recognized the voice. Rose. In a hushed tone, Carlo muttered something about water. This was followed by a warning to keep quiet.

"She'll be fine," he said. "She just needs a minute."

I could hear the rubber on her shoes as she swished away. She was...running.

"Here, lean against me," he said. "It's going to be all right. You hear me?" He had a cup of water now which he tried tipping into my mouth. I felt like a helpless baby bird. Pathetic.

"I'm sorry," I said, or tried to say.

Had I said the actual words aloud, or was it all in my mind?

Every bone in my body had turned on me.

I felt a hand come down on my cheek, quick, sharp, slapping me.

What the hell?

"Look at me," Carlo said. "You're better than this. Don't do this! Not now. Not here."

Not here.

At the station.

What am I doing?

My eyes opened, he came into focus. I looked around. We were in a room surrounded by stacks of cardboard boxes.

"I think I blacked out. Did anyone see me?"

"I don't think so," he said. "Are you feeling any better?"

"Yeah."

He handed me a cup of water. My face was wet, probably from his attempts to force the water down my throat.

"When was the last time you got some sleep?" he asked. "And by sleep, I don't mean a fifteen minute cat nap."

"Umm…maybe three, four days ago."

"I'm taking you home."

"I thought someone was driving me."

"They were," he said. "Now I am. I'm getting you home in one piece."

"Why?"

My question pained him.

"What do you mean *why?* Despite what you may think, I care. You did your best to help me. I don't want to see anyone else get hurt."

I scoffed at his last comment.

People weren't getting hurt.

They were being sent to an early grave.

Permanently.

CHAPTER 31

The ride home was somewhat of a blur. I felt weak, like I'd been drugged. I requested Maddie have access to the bodies. It wasn't common protocol to switch MEs in the middle of an investigation, but if I had the will, Carlo had the way. I also said I wanted to keep digging, keep looking, help catch the killer. He said no in a very fatherly kind of way, stating he thought it best to let his people handle the investigation from here on out. The truth of my involvement was out. I suppose he'd decided he didn't need me anymore.

At some point he seemed concerned I'd be home alone. He asked about my roommate.

Roommate.

Funny.

Cade had tried calling several times. Shelby wasn't at the station when I arrived, so I assumed he'd picked her up. Maybe they were already gone. It was probably for the best.

"Looks like someone's home," Carlo said when we arrived.

I leaned forward. He was right. The lights in my house were on. Cade's black Dodge Ram was parked on the street.

"You can...umm...let me off right here," I said.

"I don't think so," he said. "I came this far. I'll see you to the door. I'd like to do a quick check of your place before I go."

"Really, it's fine. I'll let you know if there's a—"

Problem in the form of a six foot three male wearing a cowboy hat and square-toed, leather boots, leaning against the wall in front of my doorway.

Cade spotted me in the passenger seat and was on the move.

Shit.

"Who's he?" Carlo demanded.

"The girl you met the other night at my house— he's her father. He came to pick her up."

Carlo put his window down. Cade didn't walk over. Instead he waited for me to put the window on my side down. He stuck a hand in, reached across me. "Cade McCoy."

Carlo squinted before accepting his hand, the shake between them looking like a battle of grips.

"Carlo Luciana."

"Luciana. Any relation to Giovanni Luciana?"

"He's my brother. And you—you're the detective from Wyoming, right? The one Sloane helped find those missing children last fall."

Cade nodded. "Is...everything okay?"

If I remained in the car any longer, Carlo would take the opportunity to continue asking questions.

"Look," I said to Carlo. "I appreciate the offer to put a detail on me, but I don't want it. Use them to keep an eye on someone else. I don't want another woman to go missing."

"Sloane, you need to—"

"No, Carlo. I'll be fine."

"I don't care if you want it or not. It's happening."

I opened the car door, got out, closed it behind me.

Cade slung an arm around me and looked at Carlo. "Nice to meet you."

Carlo grimaced.

It didn't matter.

I hadn't done anything wrong.

I wasn't with his brother.

Not anymore.

"I thought you might have gone home," I said.

"Couldn't leave without knowin' you was all right."

I snuck a glance at him, realizing I'd kind of missed the country boy who switched the "were" for "was" in conversation. "I wanted to call. I haven't had a moment to myself all day."

"Shelby asked if we could stay tonight, make you dinner. She feels bad about everything."

"Did you two have a chance to talk?" I asked.

"It was more of a screaming match for the first hour, but we both agreed things need to change. She needs to take more responsibility for her actions. She's almost an adult. It's time she started actin' like one."

A brisk wind sailed past. I wrapped my arms around my shoulders. Cade removed his jacket, draped it over my shoulders. Always the gentleman. We'd reached the porch, but he didn't seem ready to go in. There was movement behind the peephole on the other side of the door. Shelby.

"And you—what do you need to change?" I asked.

"It's time for me to move on."

"Move on?"

"I can't keep waitin' for Shelby's mother to come back one day."

I never knew he had been.

He looked like he wanted to eat his words. "Oh, no. It's not what you think."

"How do you know? I haven't said anything."

"It's just—you looked like you didn't understand what I meant."

"You don't owe me an explanation."

I was about to get one anyway.

"I haven't wanted my ex back for a long time. It's just…Shelby needs her. My mother does what she can, but she's gettin' older, and besides, it's not the same. Shelby needs someone to do the things I can't."

"You *can*," I said. "One decent, loving parent is far better than two dysfunctional ones."

"Sounds like you had it rough."

"There were good days and there were bad. By the time I was in high school I'd practically raised my sister, Gabrielle, all by myself. My mother did what she could. She loved us. But the abuse she received from my dad changed her as a person. She was stifled in many ways, never allowed to be her true self. And when you're not yourself, how are you supposed to raise two children?"

The front door swung open. Boo bounded out, prancing in circles around the two of us

"You two comin' in or what?" Shelby asked.

Cade looked at me. "I feel guilty, like we're invading your space. We can stay at a hotel tonight. I'm not tryin' to get in your way, especially after all you've done."

"Stay. Having you here will keep me distracted."

"To be honest, I kinda wondered if the guy in the car was Giovanni."

"Is that why you made a mad dash for the car the second we drove up?"

He grinned. "I have no idea what you mean."

I socked him in the arm.

Shelby backed inside the house with a smile on her face wider than the Brooklyn Bridge. She pushed the door closed so it was only open a crack—like there was any chance we'd believe she wasn't still listening.

"How are things with Giovanni anyway?" Cade prodded.

"They're not. He left. We're not together anymore."

"Are you—"

"Dealing with it. I have plenty of other things to worry about right now."

"I'm sorry," he said. "I should have already asked. How's it going?"

"Not tonight. You can ask me tomorrow, just not today."

"I understand."

He didn't, but I appreciated the sentiment all the same.

The smell wafting through the kitchen air, was, to be honest, not the most inviting aroma I'd ever breathed in. Shelby seemed so proud of herself, there was no way I was going to dampen her spirits. Cade, on the other hand, was a man.

"Shelby, did you burn somethin'?" he asked.

With Boo in one hand and a spatula in the other, Shelby indicated her displeasure at his criticism. "I did what the recipe said, Dad."

Emphasis on the word "Dad."

"I'm sure it will be great," I said. "I'm going to get changed."

I'd taken my top off before I became acutely aware my bedroom door wasn't shut all the way. I caught a glimpse of a boot and heard the words, "Hey, Sloane, I'm going to—" He stepped forward, took one glance, and backed out.

"The dinner, it's not going to work," he hollered through the bedroom door. "I told Shelby we'd go pick up some food and bring it back."

"You don't have to—I'm sure I have something that will work."

"We looked in your fridge. You don't."

What did he expect? Most of the time I was cooking for one.

"You have a preference?" he asked.

"No sushi. Anything else is fine. I think I'll take a bath while you're gone. I could use one."

"We won't be long," he said.

CHAPTER 32

I decided to forego the bath and opened my laptop instead. The file Butch forwarded was ready and waiting. I clicked play, and voila, *Bed of Bones* started rolling.

It began the same way Butch said it had in real life. Two boys discover a mine shaft, the youngest falling in, plunging to his untimely death. Fast forward to a swarm of detectives and cops arriving at the scene, soon learning a small boy wasn't the only thing waiting at the bottom of the mine.

I saw seven bodies in the dirt of the mine bed, all placed feet first to form a circle, their arms crossed over their chest, facing a sky they would never see. Behind their heads were gnarled-looking wooden crosses, each bearing the crude etchings Butch had spoken of before.

According to the actor playing lead detective, the women had all been taken between Draper and Salt Lake City, Utah, all within months of each other, over a span of four years. Before the gruesome discovery, there were no clues, no tips, nothing leading investigators to the abandoned mine shaft in Park City. When the women went missing, it was like they'd vanished. Every case had gone cold.

I pressed the fast-forward button on the remote and hit play again when a ranch house was displayed on the screen. I expected the scene to cut to the inside of the house where maybe police would be conducting a search, finding the typed confessions, among other things. I was wrong. Melody Sinclair had added backstory, reverting to a time when Chester Compton was still alive. I watched in disappointment. She'd recreated what she assumed had happened—a movie scenario. It was a clever idea to be sure, but since Chester was dead when they eventually linked the murders to him, there was no way most of what I was seeing could be verified.

I watched the screen. A middle-aged Chester Compton sat at a small, wooden desk, his head down, feverishly typing away on an old typewriter. The camera zoomed in on the words as his fingers pressed the keys. A scripture passage from the book of Proverbs. No big revelation there. Then justification on why *she* had to die.

Then, a door opened and a woman came in. Chester stood up, and they embraced. He said her name.

Pearl.

His wife.

Pearl gazed at the typewriter, her eyes shifting from left to right, leading one to believe she was reading the words he'd typed. This part was mere speculation on Melody Sinclair's part, pure fiction as far as I was concerned since Pearl never admitted to knowing anything about the missing women. Maybe it was this sliver of an embellishment that caused the words LYING TONGUE to appear on Melody's grave marker.

My phone buzzed.

"I've been trying to reach you for three days!"

It was Maddie. She didn't sound pleased.

"I'm sorry. My life has been a whirlwind ever since we got back."

"How is it any different than any other time?" she quipped.

"Did you talk to Carlo?" I said.

"I did."

"And?"

"At first it was a resounding *no*. Katherine Gellar, the other ME, had an absolute come apart when she found out I wanted access to the bodies. Then her son got whacked in the head by a hockey puck a few hours ago at his game. She begged them to allow her until tomorrow morning to look over the bodies."

"I'm guessing that didn't go over well," I said.

"Yeah, they want them processed now, before another woman goes missing."

"Lucky for you."

"I've downed two cans of Red Bull already. 'Lucky' isn't even close."

"You're at the lab now then?" I asked.

"*Her* lab—dealing with *her* people, but hey, I'm here, just like you wanted."

"And?"

"Interesting."

"What's interesting?" I asked.

She had a gift for leaving me hanging.

"We'll get to it. First, what questions do you have for me?"

"Were they all killed at the same time?" I asked.

"I can't be certain. Rigor and lividity is hard to determine because of the condition in which their bodies were found. I will say this...stomach contents indicate they were killed soon after they were taken. Whatever food they consumed before their abduction, it's still there."

"What do you mean?"

"The GI tract empties within twenty-four hours, but with these ladies, I can tell what their last meal was. Easiest way to explain it is the food is frozen in time along with the bodies."

"What about the gunshot wounds, anything there?"

"All three women had contact wounds, meaning the gun's muzzle was pressed against the skin when it was fired. I found significant charring on the skin surrounding the wound on all three vics."

"The wounds wouldn't happen to have been made by a forty-five?"

"How did you know?"

"I'll explain later," I said.

"With Melody Sinclair and Victoria Broderick, the bullets were through-and-through. With Brynn Rowland, the bullet's lodged inside her skull. I can see it on the x-ray."

"Can you tell if any of them fought back?"

"Melody Sinclair did. She has a few defensive wounds on her hands. They've been wiped clean though. There's nothing under the nails."

"Have we arrived at the interesting part yet?"

"Brynn Rowland."

"What about her?" I asked.

"She was pregnant."

"When he killed her?"

"No, she'd had an abortion. My guess, a few weeks ago. There's inflammation in the lining of her uterus as well as scarring in her cervical canal from where the fetus and placenta were scraped out."

I thought about the words on Brynn's grave marker: SHEDDER OF BLOOD and the scripture reference sent through text, also about shedding blood. In the verses I read to Butch at the museum it mentioned the same, the shedding of innocent blood. Innocent being the unborn child.

He knew.

The killer knew she was pregnant, which meant somehow, in some way, he either knew her or had been around her, watching, waiting.

I could think of one person who knew she was pregnant. The same person most likely to be the baby's daddy—Ronnie.

"Sloane, are you still there?"

"I'm here. Maddie, I'm sorry, I need to go."

I hung up, redialed. "I need to talk to Ronnie."

"You can't," Carlo said. "You're supposed to be resting."

"Please, it's important."

"You can't, Sloane."

"Not even if he's either the killer or may know who the killer is?"

He sighed, loud and irritated. "Let's hear it."

I told him what Maddie had just told me.

"I need to know who else knew about the pregnancy," I said, when I'd finished. "Who he told, who she told, how many people knew about it. If he acts like it's news to him, I'd say he's either lying, or he has more to do with what's happening than we thought. The person who murdered Brynn knew she'd aborted the baby."

"I'll talk to him."

"But I was hoping I could—"

"It's the only way," he said. "Get some rest."

Click.

CHAPTER 33

I'd lost my appetite by the time Cade and Shelby arrived, plastic bags in hand. They were engaged in a conversation that made me hopeful things were on the right track between father and daughter again. I'd fiddled with my phone at least a dozen times over the last several minutes, waiting and hoping Carlo would call me back. What if he didn't call me at all? I set it to the side. I needed to stop obsessing. Then I snatched it up again. Who was I kidding?

"It doesn't look like you made it into the bath," Cade pointed out.

"I was on the phone with Maddie."

"How's she doin' these days?"

"I think she's about to disown me as a friend. Otherwise, she's good."

Along with dinner, Cade presented me with a colorful array of wildflowers, carefully preserved in grocery-store plastic. It was his way of saying thank you, he said. I tried not to focus on the giant, fushia-colored, plastic heart bursting with pride from the center of the arrangement when I took them out, placing them in a vase that had once belonged to my sister. I used the flowers as an excuse to return to my room, where, in a fit of urgency I texted Carlo. If he didn't respond soon, I'd upgrade my status to stalker. I waited one minute, then two. Nothing. Any longer and Cade would wonder what was really going on, and I didn't want to worry him.

When I walked back to the kitchen, one part of the McCoy family was noticeably absent. "Where's Shelby?"

"She went to get her soda. She left it in the truck."

"How long has she been out there?"

"A few minutes maybe. I'm guessing she left it out there on purpose so she could call her boyfriend. She says she'll end it with him when we get back. We'll see."

I panicked. Something didn't feel right. I'd been jumpy all day; I needed to relax.

"What's wrong?" Cade asked.

"Nothing." I drew the curtain back with my hand, but it was too dark outside. I'd hoped if she was in the truck she'd have an interior light on. She didn't.

"What are you doing?"

"Cade...there's something I should tell you. The killer, he called me earlier today. And honestly, I have no idea if he knows where I live or not. Carlo said they were sending someone to keep an eye on me. Did you see anyone?"

"No."

"Maybe they're not here yet."

He looked at me as if to say: *Why didn't you mention this before?* He bolted. I followed. When he reached the truck he practically ripped the passenger-side door open. He reached forward, clutched the soda bottle in his hand.

Shelby wasn't in the truck.

She wasn't near the truck.

He called out for her. I called out for her.

The only sound we heard was the faint hoot of an owl in the distance.

"You don't think she took off again?"

I didn't.

"Call her," I said.

He scrambled for the phone in his pocket, dialed the number, waited.

Frantic wailing streamed through the phone. "Help me, Daddy, help me!"

"Shelby, honey. Where are you? Tell me where you are."

The line went dead.

Cade called again.

Straight to voicemail.

Again and again and again.

My pocket vibrated. "Hello?"

Breathing, heavy, just like before.

No.

It couldn't be.

But it was. The killer.

He was smart. He'd probably ditched Shelby's traceable phone, called back on his own.

I dropped to my knees, the snow seeping inside my pants, soaking me.

Cade took the phone from my hand, yelled one threat after the other.

"Put the woman back on," a scruffy male voice interrupted. "The female detective."

Cade ignored the demand, continued his rant.

The man said, "Put her on or I hang up in five...four...three...two..."

Cade crouched down, held the phone out in front of me.

"I'm here," I said.

"Are you listening?"

"Yes."

"Good."

"Why have you taken her?" I asked. "I don't understand. She has nothing to do with the movie."

"I talk. You listen."

The idea of being subservient to such a ruthless killer disgusted me. But I had no choice. Cade, on the other hand, saw it another way.

"Where's my daughter, you sick freak?!" Cade's voice boomed through the softness of night.

"Tell the father to simmer down," the man said. "Tell him...or this call is over."

I flipped on an interior light in Cade's truck, popped open the jockey box, jerked out a pen and a semi-used napkin. I scribbled: CALL CARLO; GO FIND HER.

I shot out of the truck, raced toward the house, tore apart the dresser inside my room. I found my Bible and opened it, feverishly turning the pages. The Sundance Killer had Shelby, and if his intention was to take her life, I needed to play along, or she wouldn't live long enough to see tomorrow.

"Her father's gone," I said. "It's just me. I'm listening."

I sounded out of breath. I'm sure he knew it.

Dead air.

"I know why you bombed the theater," I said. "I know why you took the women. I know why you killed them."

"Do you understand now—do you see?"

"I do."

"Tell me what you understand."

"They're wicked," I said. "All of them. They needed to die."

"You're lying. You're just trying to appease me."

"A woman who kills her unborn baby, a child with the right to life, she deserves to die."

I was careful not to use Brynn's name—I wanted him to believe she was no more human to me than she was to him. It pained me to speak of her in such an unfeeling way, but I had no choice.

"Tell me more."

His voice was heightened—he was curious. What I'd said pleased him.

"She took a life so you took hers," I said. "I believe in karma. Don't you?"

"And the others?"

I had theories as to why Melody Sinclair died, but if I got it wrong now, I risked everything.

"She made a movie filled with lies," I said.

"What lies did she tell?"

This was the part I feared the most. I took a deep breath. *Please be right.* "The movie. Some of it was fact, some of it was fiction. You couldn't allow anyone to see it—not until it was right. Not until everyone could know the real truth."

"Tell me, what is the *real truth?*"

He sounded agitated now. He was testing me. I needed to do something, say something, convince him I understood...even though I didn't and never would.

"Chester's wife. She didn't know anything, did she?"

The way he laughed let me know my answer was lacking. "Dig harder. You still don't see. You don't get the most important part. Do you know why I took the girl?"

He'd switched subjects on me. I wanted to say: Who are the other four? When are you taking them? But I couldn't. I had to focus on Shelby. I had to give her value. I had to make her real.

"I interrupted your process," I said. "There are four others still living in sin. I didn't know you weren't finished."

"Then why did you do it? Why stop me? If you believe, why interrupt me, Sloane Monroe? Why? Why? Why?!"

"I wasn't trying to keep you from doing your work. I wanted to see them. I wanted to see you."

I wanted to vomit.

"Why did you take Shelby?" I asked. "Shelby doesn't fit your code. Shelby has nothing to do with the movie. Shelby knows nothing of the story. Shelby is different. She's not like the others. It's the mother you want, not her."

Shelby, Shelby, Shelby. I would keep saying her name until she mattered to him.

"Her mother—why?"

I had his attention. Good.

"Shelby's mother left her. She abandoned her. She gave her up."

"Why should I care?"

"Because Shelby's innocent. Give her back, take me instead."

"You'd trade your life for hers? Why would I want *you?*"

"It's me you're trying to punish," I said. "I'm the reason the one place you care about the most has been trampled upon. You're angry with me. You want to teach me a lesson, so you took Shelby. I have a lesson for you too."

"Which is...?"

"Withhold not correction from the child: for if thou beatest her with the rod, she shall not die."

I'd replaced the "he" for "she," knowing he'd understand.

"Proverbs?"

"23 and 13, yes. Just tell me when and where. I'll come alone."

I said it with no hesitation, no reserve.

He answered with a scripture of his own. "She openeth her mouth with wisdom; and in her tongue is the law of kindness."

The line went dead.

And I knew. He couldn't take me. As much as I had pained him by seeking him out, by destroying the sickening thing he found so dear, in his own way, he respected me for it. What that meant for Shelby, I didn't know.

For as young as she was, she had her wits about her. I bowed my head and prayed in silence. *Please let us find her alive. Please.*

CHAPTER 34

Within ten minutes an overabundance of officers and agents converged, their vehicles lining both sides of my block. Given the late hour, lights came on at every neighboring house but one. At the house two doors down, a curtain was drawn back with the slightest of movements. My neighbor, a widower in his late eighties, probably assumed at such a snail's pace, no one would ever notice. I did. He'd broken one of the cardinal rules of spying—forgetting to turn the light off in the room first. It was too dark out for me to ascertain what he was looking at, but since I was standing directly under a street lamp, I waved anyway. The curtain thrust closed.

Sleep well, Mr. Fuller.

A BOLO alert had been issued with Shelby's description. Under the direction of Carlo, the scene surrounding my house was processed under a black sky. The elements didn't make the job any easier, but we had one thing to be thankful for: it wasn't snowing. Everyone was given a task. Some dusted for prints; others collected anything they considered to be viable evidence. Footprints in the snow led halfway to Cade's truck then appeared to drag backward, meeting a set of tire marks I was sure would match the ones we'd found at the start of the road where the three bodies were located.

An hour passed, then two. One by one my street became quiet again.

Cade returned, a look of desperation on his face. He joined me in the house where I had just finished going over the phone call I'd received from the Sundance Killer. Cade leaned against a wall in my dining room, his head down, one boot crossed over the other. He hadn't said a word since he came inside. I imagined he was torn apart. I wanted to go to him, offer some words of comfort, but I held back, giving him the space he needed.

I thought about the phone call. The first time I'd spoken to the killer, adrenaline and panic had stopped me from listening, hearing him. Not his words but his voice. This time, I detected something in his tone, something familiar, almost like I'd heard it before.

Carlo's phone rang. He rounded the corner, entered my bedroom, and shut the door. I heard his voice, but couldn't make out what was being said.

I couldn't remain still any longer. I walked over to Cade, placed my hands inside his, rubbed his palms with my thumbs. "Are you all right?"

He lifted his head and looked at me, his face damp, red. We stood together, eyes locked on each other for some time before he said in a low voice, "She's my whole life. She's all I've got. I can't lose her. I just can't."

I heard footsteps in the hall. Carlo glanced at my hands, seeing they were interlocked with Cade's. I didn't let go. He looked past me at Cade and smiled. "She's at the station."

A mixture of shock and relief flowed through me. "Shelby?"

Carlo nodded.

"I can't believe it!" Cade said.

Neither could I.

"How did she get there?" Cade asked.

"He let her go."

"He just drove into the police station, let her out, and drove away?" Cade asked.

"Chief Sheppard said she came walking through the door a few minutes ago, black pillowcase in hand. She told the chief that the man put it over her head when he took her. He released Shelby about a block away from the station, told her to count to fifty Mississippi's and then she could remove the cover from her head. He said if she took it off early, he'd blow her head off."

"I don't understand," Cade said. "Why would he take her then let her go? It doesn't make sense."

In a sick, twisted way, it did to me.

"He was angry," I said. "When he took her, he knew he couldn't kill her. He doesn't know her enough to justify her death. She's not part of the seven."

"I agree," Carlo said. "The way we've profiled him, we believe he planned his kills way ahead of time. He knew who he was taking and when...and why. With Shelby, he acted out of character, making a rash decision out of spite." He looked at me. "Sloane, I think he's convinced himself he's extended an olive branch with Shelby. He gives her back, you leave him alone...maybe even hoping he's convinced us to leave him alone, especially if he doesn't believe what he's doing is wrong."

I hoped Carlo was right. I wanted the killer to be vulnerable, not looking over his shoulder. I wanted to catch him when he least expected it.

"You," Cade said, looking at me. "*You* saved her life, Sloane. What you said on the phone, you must have convinced him to let her go."

I didn't feel like a hero. I hadn't saved the day. If it wasn't for me, Shelby wouldn't have been taken in the first place.

"She's safe now," I said.

And I was determined never to put her life in danger again.

CHAPTER 35

Shelby told investigators she'd gone out to her father's truck to get her soda and could hear a shuffling sound, like someone was creeping up behind her. She glanced back, thinking it was her dad not wanting to let her out of his sight. A wide piece of tape was slapped over her mouth, followed by thin fabric coming down over her face. She couldn't see out. An object, cool and hard, pressed against the fabric, pushing in, resting on the back of her head. The barrel of a gun. She knew this because he'd told her.

When the man shoved her into his truck, he'd seized her by the arm, said if she made a sound, any sound at all, he'd enter the house, killing her father first before turning the gun on me. When she nodded in understanding, he demanded she sit on the floor, in front of the seat, low enough so no one could see her. She was told to bring her knees to her chest, cross her arms in front of them, and leave them there unless he said otherwise.

They'd driven in silence for several minutes, the bag remaining on her head. Then her cell phone rang, at which time he'd cranked the steering wheel, taking them to the side of the road, and got out. The moment he left the truck, she'd lifted the bag up a few inches, answered the call.

The man wrestled the phone away from her, hurled it on the ground. She heard the heel of his shoe come down, smashing the phone into pieces. She thought she'd die for her disobedience. Then he did something she didn't expect. He took out his own phone and dialed. She stayed quiet, listened to the sound of his voice, deep and raspy. He didn't sound young, like a boy her age, but he wasn't old either. His truck reeked of chewing tobacco.

While the man talked on the phone, Shelby did what any curious teen would do, she felt around, slowly moving her fingers across the carpet beneath her. It was clean. No wrappers, no trash, nothing.

The man ended the phone call, wrenched her arm, set her on the seat next to him. She swung her hand around, clawed at the skin on his arm. He swore, struck her in the face. Then it got weird. He asked her if she would tell him a story. He wanted to know why her mother had left. Shelby was smart enough to hear the sympathy in his voice when he made the request. He told her he wanted to know everything, from beginning to end. She brought herself to tears as she mixed truth with lies, painting her mother as a modern-day Cruella de Vil. And it had worked.

When she finished talking, he'd battered his fists on the steering wheel. He commanded Shelby to return to the floorboard once again. He put the truck in gear and drove to a house. She knew this because she heard a garage door go up. They transferred from the truck to a car. The car smelled like lavender inside. They drove out of the garage, and the garage door went down. He drove several minutes then stopped again. He asked her to hold out her hands.

He didn't *tell* her.

He *asked* her.

He then scrubbed her hands and fingernails with a wet cloth. It smelled like hand sanitizer, but stronger. He gave her specific instructions which he made her repeat before reaching in front of her, opening the passenger side door, and letting her go.

As Shelby told her story, every person witnessing her statement was baffled.

To my left, a short female rushed toward me, flailing her arms. She entered the interrogation room. "We found something when we were processing the girl's coat."

All eyes shifted to the woman and the white Ziploc dangling from her hand. A single slip of paper was inside. "This note was shoved inside the girl's pocket."

The chief turned to Shelby, eyes wide. "You know about this?"

"How could I? There was a bag over my head."

"You have no idea when it was put there?"

"Umm...like I said... *no.*"

Emphasis on the "no."

The chief held the bag in front of him, read aloud. "Proverbs 28:10 Whoso causeth the righteous to go astray in an evil way, he shall fall himself into his own pit; but the upright shall have good *things* in possession."

This one was different. It didn't fit. What message was he sending, and to whom?

Before we left, I took Carlo aside, pressing him about whether they'd spoken to Ronnie about Brynn.

"We did," Carlo said. "Get this. He didn't deny she had the abortion. He knew about the baby, but he claims it wasn't his."

"I thought they were a couple?" I asked.

"A few months ago, they took a break. The way Ronnie tells it, the break was Brynn's idea. They got back together a month ago, and she confessed she'd had a one-night stand."

"Did she say who with?"

"He told her he didn't want to know. In his opinion, she only told him because she found out she was pregnant and she wanted to keep the baby. He said the only way he'd take her back was if she got rid of it."

"Nice," I said. "I guess carrying the baby to term and giving it up for adoption to a loving couple desperate to have a child of their own was out of the question."

"He claims he was embarrassed. He didn't want anyone to know what she had done. He said they couldn't be together again until the deed was done, and if he found out she'd told anyone, even one of her friends, they were over for good."

"So she had the abortion," I said. "And he has no idea who the father is or was. Terrific."

"Were you thinking the Sundance Killer was the father?"

"No. None of the victims had been violated sexually. In my opinion, he sees them as unclean. It was probably random, and while he was hunting Brynn, he found out about it somehow."

"I agree."

An image emerged in my head of the Sundance Killer—a silent predator, lurking, following, hiding in the shadows. Waiting and watching for months, maybe even longer. His obsession growing day after day as he monitored the movie. Disruption or not, he'd keep going. He was three down, and there were still four more to go.

CHAPTER 36

I wouldn't have blamed Cade for splitting as soon as he was given permission to take his daughter, but he didn't. He asked to stay another night. It was late. The roads back to Jackson Hole would be icy. It was safer if he left in the morning.

It took a couple hours, but with the help of a sleep aid, Boo snuggled by her side, and the kind of comfort only her father could give, Shelby finally dozed off.

After Cade had suffered through the loss of his daughter twice in one week, I decided it was only fair to answer his questions, starting with the explosion on day one and going from there. By the time I finished, he knew as much as I did. It felt good to let it all out. I ended the conversation by expressing how sorry I was.

Again.

It was a word I had become an expert at saying.

"You don't need to keep apologizin' for everything. Do you think I haven't ever lost someone on a case I was workin'? We never want these things to happen.

Sometimes they just do. As a friend, I'm tellin' you right now, it's time you get an alarm system installed in this house. I don't wanna hear about your guns either. Sometimes guns aren't enough. Not with the kind of cases you take on."

He was right.

"I'll think about it," I said.

"I don't want you to think about it, I want you to do it. If it's too much hassle, I'll install it myself before I leave."

"I appreciate the offer, but I'm sure you can't wait to get out of here. I'm glad you stayed tonight. It makes me feel a lot better knowing you're here."

"Even with the officer across the street?"

For a minute, I'd forgotten the officer was there. Most people would feel safe knowing an officer of the law was outside their home, specifically assigned for their protection. Instead, I felt trapped.

"I don't know him," I said, "the officer in the squad car. I know you. There's the difference."

"You think you'll hear from him again?"

"The killer?" I asked.

"Him too, I guess. But I was talkin' about Giovanni."

I wondered when Giovanni would come up again.

"He…chose his family."

"I don't understand. Why?"

"His father put him in a position, forced him to make a choice," I said.

"You don't seem surprised."

"I'm not. It's almost like I expected this to happen."

"Why?"

"Our relationship had been strained lately."

"Do you regret it?"

"What?" I asked.

"Callin' it quits."

It was a loaded question, and it deserved a careful, well thought-out answer. I resisted the urge to blurt out my initial thought, knowing I couldn't unsay something once it had been said. I didn't want to admit a fragment of my heart felt like it had been severed from me. I didn't want to reveal I'd considered calling Giovanni several times over the last two days, once even dialing his number and then hanging up before it started to ring. Those kinds of admissions were embarrassing, and not the kind another guy wanted to hear, no matter what they said to the contrary. No straight man remains close to a woman only to be content in the role of friend. Anyone who says different is lying, to themselves and to the other person. In my world, whether they admitted it or not, men wanted all or nothing.

"I try not to live my life with regrets," I said. "I'm a realist. I accept things the way they are, learn from my mistakes, move on." A good, safe answer, except he wasn't buying it. I could tell. I'd never been much of a salesperson.

"You should go to bed. Your eyes are startin' to close."

"No they're not. I'm fine."

He leaned forward, framing my face with his hand. "Trust me, they are."

I stood.

"Do you need more blankets? Another pillow? Anything?" I asked.

He kicked off his boots, set them to the side, pulled his hat over his face.

"You're sleeping in your clothes?" I asked.

"Nope," he said through the hat. "I'm just waitin' for you."

The thought of him dressed in anything other than Western wear was amusing.

"What time are you thinking you'll head out in the morning?"

"We'll see."

We'll see. Noncommittal.

I walked over, pulled the hat off his face. "Cade?"

"Yeah?"

"You *are* leaving, right?"

"Why'd you ask—you want me to?"

"I didn't say—"

"Sounds like it."

"You're avoiding the question," I said.

"And you're avoidin' sleep." He pulled the hat back over his face. "Goodnight, Sloane."

CHAPTER 37

The time on my wall clock said it was a little past eleven in the morning, which couldn't have been right. I never slept past seven. Maybe the batteries were dead. I reached for my cell phone, hoping the clock was wrong. No such luck.

I wrapped my hair around an elastic band, brushed my teeth, and did my best to walk a straight line to the living room. My head was pounding. Too little sleep followed by too much does wonders for a person. Cade sat on a chair, feet propped up on the coffee table, eyes glued to a hunting show on the television on a channel I never knew I had. Three men, dressed in camouflage from head to toe, crouched down, rifles in hand, all of them whispering.

"What's with the lowered voices?" I asked.

Cade turned around, tried not to seem startled to find me standing there, even though he was. "They don't want the animals knowin' they're there."

He was whispering too. Odd.

"What animals?"

Before he could answer, one of the guys stuck a small device in between his lips. He squeezed it then blew into the hole. It emitted a sound so shrill, I imagined a chipmunk screaming.

"They're callin' in a coyote."

"Using that…thing? I thought they were trying to be quiet?"

My lack of intelligence in the area of hunting seemed to amuse him.

"It's supposed to sound like a rabbit."

"A rabbit doing what?" I asked.

"Uhh…dyin'…the sound brings 'em in."

I wasn't sure what face I pulled, but the TV was switched off without delay.

"There's no rabbit," he said. "It's just a device. Okay?"

"Yep."

"You hungry?"

He walked to the kitchen, uncovered a plate of eggs, bacon, potatoes, even toast.

"When did you get all of this?" I asked.

"Last night. We stopped at the store before all the madness happened."

I bit into a piece of bacon and revisited my question from the night before. "So when do you plan on heading out?"

"Let's talk about it."

"About what?" I asked.

"Leaving."

"Why? What's wrong?"

"I'm not going anywhere."

"What do you mean?" I asked.

"This guy you're lookin' for...when he took my daughter, he made it personal."

"They'll catch him."

"Maybe they will or maybe *I* will. I don't give a damn if I don't have jurisdiction here. I'm not leavin'."

There was no point trying to talk him out of it. I knew he wouldn't listen. I opened my mouth to object then closed it. Having him stay wasn't such a bad thing. I just needed to keep us both under the radar.

"What are your plans today?" he asked. "You're still goin' after him, right?"

I shot him a wink. "Do you really have to ask?"

...

I stood in Maddie's living room giving her my best "I need your help" stare. I used it often. She recognized it right away.

"What's going on?" she asked.

"I need a favor."

Maddie gave Shelby a once over. "I can tell."

"I dig your...house," Shelby said. "It's so...orange, and bright, and colorful."

Maddie had never been one to adhere to any specific trend. Her living room walls might have been adorned with massive orange-and-white flowered prints, with an accent wall in the brightest hue of hot pink, but her bedroom was another story. It was black and decorated in a spicy shade of red that men couldn't resist. It made her relationship with the straight-as-an-arrow Chief Sheppard seem even more surreal to me. I supposed everyone had secret fantasies. Even him.

"I live alone which means I can do whatever I want," Maddie boasted. "That's the beauty of flying solo."

"Sloane lives alone," Shelby said. "Her house doesn't look like this."

Maddie and Shelby laughed in unison. Nice.

"I dig your outfit," Maddie said.

Shelby blushed. I'd made the right decision bringing her here.

Cade, who'd skipped the pleasantries, stared with an intense fascination at Maddie's DVD collection. He looked different today, surprising me by slipping on a ball cap instead of his usual hat, which made him look like a bull rider at a summer rodeo. In a ball cap and a button-up shirt with frayed pockets, he reminded me a lot of the country singer, Eric Church. Not bad. Not bad at all.

"Madison, good to see you again," Cade said.

"Is this cute one yours?" She nodded at Shelby.

He raised a brow indicating "cute" depended on the day. "She is."

Maddie looked back at me. "What do you two need from me?"

"Can Shelby hang out here today, if you're not working?" I asked.

"I need to go in for a while. I'll take her with me." Maddie looked at me then placed a hand on her hip. "What, you're afraid of her seeing a few dead people? I'm sure she can handle it."

Maddie didn't understand why anyone wouldn't be fascinated by deceased bodies on a coroner's table.

"Can I talk to you for a minute?" I asked.

We walked into the other room.

"Calm down," Maddie scolded. "Don't be so paranoid. I won't let her anywhere near the dearly departed if it's a problem. She can hang out with my assistants, watch them process stuff."

"How much do you know about what happened to Shelby?" I asked.

"I'd know a lot more if you returned my phone calls."

"Maddie…"

"Wade stayed over last night. I know all about it anyway."

"This guy, he let her go," I said. "I'm not worried he'll come after her again. I just don't want her to be alone, and Cade insists on going with me."

"Since when did you allow a guy to insist on anything?"

"The killer took his daughter. He has a right to go after him."

"I got it. She'll be fine. Go. I'll talk to you later."

CHAPTER 38

"Where to?" Cade asked once we'd returned to the car.

"When I met with Butch he told me they'd had a robbery at the museum awhile back. He thought one of his female employees was behind it, but he didn't have enough proof."

"What do you know about her?"

"He gave me her name. Karin Ackerman."

"Do you know where to find her?"

Silly question.

"She has a yoga studio over in Kimball Junction."

"And she's there now?" he asked.

"She's just finishing her last class and is getting ready to start another one."

"Let me guess—with you?"

"I've requested a private session."

"What would you like me to do?" he asked.

We turned in front of Tranquility Yoga and parked. I tugged the nylon cord on my duffle bag in the back seat, leaned over, and patted Cade on the shoulder.

"Would you wait here? If she's a runner, I might need back up."

As a detective in Jackson Hole, Wyoming, he was used to giving orders, not taking them. But the odds of him taking a yoga class were slim to never-in-this-lifetime.

I entered the building, changed into more suitable clothes, and found Karin sitting on a mat. Her slim yet muscular legs were folded one over the other. Her hair was in a fishtail braid cascading down the side of her neck. Her hands were pressed together, head down, eyes closed. She was either meditating or praying. Several feet in front of her was a basket filled with rolled mats. I took one, sat down, bent my knees, waited.

"You haven't ever done yoga before, have you?" Karin asked. Her eyelids fluttered open like she'd awakened from a deep sleep.

"Jujitsu mostly. Is it obvious?"

"Your posture is a bit...off."

I hadn't the slightest idea what she was talking about. My posture was perfect.

"I've been meaning to branch out, try something new," I said.

It was true. I'd received a red-and-black belt, accomplishing my goal in mixed martial arts.

"What do you know about yoga?"

"Not much," I said. "I've heard it's relaxing."

"Depends on what kind you do."

We began the session with some deep breathing and then moved into some restorative poses, focusing on relaxation. I wanted to get right down to business, ask my questions, but I found myself enjoying the way I felt. The tightness in my body diminished, my stress faded.

We stood and began sun salutations followed by something she called "tree pose." I shifted my weight to the right, bent my knee, lifted my left leg off the ground, and rested it on my inner thigh, my toe pointed toward the floor. She asked me to fix my gaze on an object in the room and hold it there. Once we mirrored each other in balance, the questioning began.

"Am I allowed to talk?" I asked.

"Do you need a break?"

"I like the pose. It's just hard for me to stay quiet this long."

In real life, I preferred to sit back, remain a quiet observer. On the job, it was a different story.

"You'll get used to it. I'd rather you stay quiet, try to focus." Her eyes were steadfast, unmoving.

"I got your number from a girl I met at the Park City Museum," I said.

The statement didn't seem to rattle her in the least. My delivery was lacking. I tried a more direct approach.

"The girl I met told me she'd gone to the museum when she heard the indie film *Bed of Bones* was coming to the Sundance Film Festival this year."

No movement. "I'm not familiar with it."

Although still, I believed her statement. She didn't seem to have a clue what I was talking about. *Did she own a television?*

"*Bed of Bones* was the film they shut down after the bomb went off in the theater."

She frowned. "Sad. Very sad."

She was doing a good job keeping her answers brief.

"Yeah, I didn't know what the movie was about until the girl told me it was based on a serial killer who committed several murders in this area."

"Murders?"

I had her attention. Now to keep it.

"I guess the movie was about a boy who died after falling into a mine shaft. When they went in to recover the body, they found a bunch of dead bodies down there. The girl said the museum used to have several artifacts relating to the murders, but they were stolen."

"Hmm. Too bad."

For such a relaxed pose, she was sweating.

Good.

"I guess now the movie has become national news and police have reopened the investigation, you know, to figure out what really happened. I heard they think the person who robbed the museum might be the same person who bombed the theater."

Her leg wobbled, her focus lost. She tipped, but held her arms to the side, stopping herself from toppling over.

I had an urge to pat myself on the back. It was, after all, a splendid performance.

"Oops, I know you said I should focus," I said. "Should we try the pose again? I promise I'll keep quiet this time."

"I...I'm not feeling well. I'm sorry. Would you...can we postpone?"

She started rolling up her mat before I had the chance to reply. I walked over, held out my hand. "Here, I'll put it away for you."

"No, really. It's fine. I got it. Why don't you go? I'll call you."

"I don't think so," I said.

I ripped the rolled up yoga mat from her hands, held it out in front of me. The look on her face said a lot of things, but she didn't say a word. What if word got out that the Zen yoga instructor lost her cool? It wouldn't bode well.

She stood there, staring. I had to admit, I enjoyed the empowerment.

"You worked at the museum a couple years ago, didn't you?" I asked.

"I work here."

"You do *now.*"

"Who told you I worked there?"

"Walter Thornton. Or maybe you know him as Butch. You remember him, right?"

She gauged the distance between where we stood and the door, a mere twenty feet away.

"Don't," I said. "Don't do it, Karin."

The warning was one-hundred-percent selfish on my part. I hadn't realized how sore I was after a few short minutes of stretching. Yoga was far more challenging than it appeared. And I didn't want to run. Not right now. Too bad I didn't always get what I wanted.

Karin broke into a sprint, her body colliding with a brick wall named Cade McCoy, who had impeccable timing.

"Answer the question," he said.

Karin's expression resembled a terror-stricken, wild bird locked inside a cage.

I eased up.

"Can I get you some water or something?" I asked.

"You weren't here for the class, were you?"

"I've been meaning to try yoga," I said, "but no."

"Who are you?"

I offered my name.

"I know you broke into the museum after your shift one night. I know you took everything from the display. I can take you to the police right now, or you can give back what you stole. You give it to me, we'll leave, and we won't tell anyone."

"I can't."

"Yes, you can," Cade chimed in.

"And you will," I said. "Right now. We'll escort you to your house if necessary."

"No, I mean I really can't. I don't have any of it."

"So you admit you took items that didn't belong to you?"

"Yes, but not for the reasons you think."

"Why then?" I asked.

Karin grabbed a yoga mat back out of the basket, snapped it open, sat down. "My head is spinning. I need to sit."

It seemed awkward, but we joined her on the floor.

"After I left the museum one night, I was met at my car by a man."

"Describe him," I said.

"Older. Early seventies, maybe. Normally I would have maced the guy in the face, but he was frail and weak. I didn't see him as a threat."

"What did he want?"

"Everything from Chester Compton's display. He said if I got it for him, he'd pay me five thousand dollars. Cash. You have to understand, I'm not a thief, but I'd been saving for three years to open this studio. Five thousand would give me the rest of the money I needed."

"Justifying it doesn't make it right," Cade said.

"Did you at least ask him why?" I asked.

"I tried. He said it never belonged in the museum in the first place. The way he talked about it, you would think the items were his, but almost everything we had was donated. Most of it had been taken as evidence after the murder and was released to the museum as part of the town's history."

"What were his terms?" I asked.

"The five thousand was a one-time deal. In exchange, I wasn't to ask any questions. I had two days to complete the job. He told me to wear gloves and to keep the lights off when I did it. There were huge windows in the place, so he advised me to stick to a flashlight, not turn on the lights."

"Where did you make the exchange?" I asked.

"In the museum parking lot, same as before."

244 C h e r y l   B r a d s h a w

"And after?"

"I was paid. He told me he wanted me to continue working at the museum for a couple months to avoid suspicion. Then I was to quit. If anyone asked questions, I was to deny knowing anything about it."

"Butch suspected you," I said. "He knew."

"I know. It was the longest two months of my life. I felt a tremendous amount of guilt for what I'd done."

"Not enough for you to come clean though," I said.

"If I had, I'd only have incriminated myself. I had no idea who the man was. I'd never seen him before, and I never saw him after. I didn't think anyone would believe me."

"Karin, how much do you know about what happened all those years ago?" I asked.

"Everything. Butch made us sit in on a presentation before we unveiled it to the public so we'd be able to answer most questions thrown our way."

"I'm going to tell you something the public doesn't know yet," I said. "And it needs to stay between us. Do you understand?"

She bobbed her shoulders up and down. "Sure, okay."

"I mean it. If I have to come back here because you blabbed to someone about what we talked about today, no amount of mace will keep you safe enough from me."

She rolled her eyes. "I get it."

"The murders are happening again," I said.

"What…what do you mean?"

"Three women were found yesterday, dead, their bodies frozen."

"Where?"

"Same location where the other women were found in the fifties."

"How? The mine shafts are sealed now."

"This time the women were arranged above ground."

"It can't be. Chester Compton is dead."

"Someone else is trying hard to keep his memory alive."

She cupped a hand over her mouth like she was experiencing a wave of nausea.

"I need you to think back," I said. "Try to remember the times you met with this guy. If there's anything you can tell me, anything you can remember, I need to know right now."

She curled her toes, stared at the floor. "There is one thing. He had a familiar looking face."

"Familiar…like someone you've seen before?"

"Not alive, no. One of the items we had on display at the museum was a newspaper clipping. Chester

Compton's face was on the front page. That's who he looked like."

CHAPTER 39

Willie Compton.

Grandson of Chester Compton.

Could he be alive?

Did insanity run in the family?

I did some quick math on my fingers, guesstimating Willie would be somewhere around seventy years old now. This gave me every reason to believe he was alive and kicking. Maybe Willie had returned to Park City, or maybe he'd been living here all along. I needed to find out, and fast.

If Willie masterminded the killings, he hadn't done it alone. The gruff, headstrong man I spoke to on the phone was younger by at least twenty years or more. I tried to piece it all together, make it fit, but there were holes in my theory.

I phoned an old real estate contact named Bridget Peters. A couple years earlier, I'd saved her from having her throat slashed by a money-hungry woman she'd once considered a friend. Since then Bridget had become a broker and opened up a real estate office. I was curious if Willie owned any homes in the area. She said she'd look into it and get back to me.

I made a left at the next street, headed toward the mountains.

"May I ask where we're goin'?" Cade asked.

"Chester Compton had a ranch up here. No one lives in the house anymore, but I want to take a look at it anyway."

Finding evidence at Chester's Compton's ranch, sitting there, waiting for me, wouldn't happen. It was a dead-end. Investigators had picked it apart. Twice. But I hadn't heard back from Bridget. And I didn't have any better ideas.

At the entrance to the Compton place, logs had been erected in front of the gate. In the center, a round piece of wood dangled from two weathered chains. In the center of the piece of wood, a "C" had been carved.

We arrived at the worn-down ranch house to find my suspicions were right. The property was as deserted as a 1990s drive-in. I expected the house to match the rustic property it sat on. It didn't. With four white pillars lining the front and a fireplace on each side of the two-story home, it looked like something out of *Gone with the Wind.* The colonial style had been the wife's decision, no doubt. I jiggled the handle on the front door. It was unlocked. I entered.

"What are you hopin' to find?" Cade asked.

"I just wanted to get a feel for the place. We're here, why not?"

The inside of the house was almost the same temperature as the outside, making me wish I'd added a few more layers to my ensemble. I looked around. Few furnishings remained. A striped hide-a-bed, littered with mice droppings and rips, sat in an otherwise empty living room. There were holes in the walls, the floor, and the ceiling. Even so, I imagined in its day, it was a spectacular sight to behold. Now it had been left to rot, just like Chester Compton.

Cade explored the main level while I went upstairs. I crossed my arms in front of my chest as I ascended, fearing if I nudged the railing, remnants of the ceiling the railing was attached to would spill down on top of me. The idea of a decade's worth of dust sprinkling into my hair wasn't appealing.

My phone sounded when I reached the top of the stairs. It was Carlo. I didn't want to answer, but I did anyway.

"How'd you do it?" He sounded agitated.

"Do what?"

"Sneak out? I got a call from Officer Jennings this morning saying when he knocked on your door, you didn't answer."

"It's not hard to slip past a cop in a patrol car when he's sleeping," I said.

"Son of a...Are you kidding? Where are you?"

"Out. And you don't need to send someone to look for me. I'm fine."

"You're so stubborn, Sloane."

A commendable quality.

"I have my own back up," I said. "So tell the sleeper thanks, but no thanks. We're just fine without him."

"*We* meaning the hot-shot detective from Wyoming? He hasn't left yet?"

I wasn't sure what to say, so I said nothing.

"Where are you, really?" he said. "The Sundance Killer is insane. Don't think just because you got Shelby back he won't harm you."

"He won't come after me, Carlo."

"He *will* murder again, and soon."

It wasn't what he said, it was how he said it that startled me. "What's happened?"

"Nothing. Don't worry."

"Tell me."

"All right," he said. "Give me your location and I will."

Too easy. There was a good chance he wouldn't tell me after he got what he wanted. But I'd started going numb from the cold air. I saw no reason to stay.

"I'm at the ranch house. Chester Compton's."

"We've searched every inch of his place. Why are you there?"

"I don't know."

As a private investigator, I didn't always share every piece of information I had with the long arm of the law. Sure, it meant I failed to cooperate. I suppose it was my civil duty to be forthcoming with regard to potential evidence, but in the past I'd learned there were some things you offered and other things you didn't—not until you were sure they'd lead somewhere. It kept others from pilfering my leads. And besides, I'd never shared well with others.

"The Compton place is a dead end," Carlo said. "So I'll ask again—what are you doing there?"

"Wasting my time. We're leaving."

"And going where next?"

I didn't know yet.

"I told you where I am. If you want the valuable information I was given this morning, tell me what's happened."

The tables had turned. Now to see how badly the squirrel wanted the nut.

There was a long pause, followed by a hefty sigh.

"A fourth woman is missing. We believe the killer has her."

"Shouldn't every female with the slightest connection to the movie be under police protection?"

"Not this one," he said.

"Why?"

"The girl's name is Angela Rivers. She has nothing to do with the movie itself. We didn't know about her."

"She's connected to something or someone."

"Angela Rivers was Brynn Rowland's best friend. She arrived yesterday from Los Angeles. Brynn had given Angela tickets to see the movie before she left. We don't think she knows Brynn is dead."

"What makes you think the killer took her?"

"Her rental car was found abandoned on the side of the road. It had a flat tire, and the driver's-side window was smashed in. The car doors were locked. We think she got the flat after stopping somewhere, probably courtesy of our killer. When he came up behind her, it's possible she saw him and locked the door."

"It could be him, but if she wasn't part of the movie, there would have to be something else to make you think there's a connection to the other killings."

"Taped to the steering wheel of her rental car we found another scripture reference. Proverbs 6:14:

Frowardness is in her heart, she deviseth mischief continually; she soweth discord. We looked it up. It's exact except he replaced the "he" for "she".

"Soweth discord. It makes me wonder."

"What?"

"Whether she knew Brynn was pregnant. She must have. Up to now he's only taken women affiliated with the movie. Have you processed the car yet?"

"Same as always. We found nothing." He paused. "Your turn."

"I have reason to believe Willie Compton had someone steal the artifacts from the museum, the ones relating to the original murders."

"William Compton? Chester's grandson?"

"Yes." I gave him a short, one-minute speech explaining what Butch told me about the break-in. "Based on what we know about the killer, Willie's too old."

"Unless he has help," he said. "Maybe he has kids. Hell, maybe the whole family is certifiable."

"We need to find him. Whether he's involved or not, I believe he knows something."

"If he did take her, you don't have much time."

"That's not our only problem," he said. "We notified the families of the victims last night. One of them was irate enough to run their mouth to the press."

"You knew you couldn't keep it quiet forever. At least people know Melody is innocent. Maybe it's a good thing."

"The last thing I wanted to do was give this asshole any media attention."

A call beeped in. Bridget.

The Compton ranch in Park City had been passed down to Willie when his father died, but he also owned a townhouse in Bountiful, Utah, about an hour away. Halfway through writing down the address, I heard voices downstairs. At first I assumed Carlo had either sent someone over or had been en route while we were on the phone together. Then someone shouted, "Stay where you are! Don't move!"

And it wasn't Cade.

CHAPTER 40

I crept down the timeworn stairs, my gun drawn. Halfway down I caught a glimpse of Cade. He stood in the living room, hands up, facing an older man with white hair. The white-haired man was dressed in denim overalls. He had a rifle pointed at Cade's chest.

"Who are you?" the man shouted. "Why are you here?"

"You first," Cade replied.

"I have a right to know why you're in my house. You're not dressed like a cop. So who are ya?"

Bountiful, Utah, had come to me. How convenient.

"His name is Cade McCoy," I said. "Mine is Sloane Monroe. He's a detective, I'm a PI."

A caught-off-guard Willie Compton shifted in my direction just enough to acknowledge my gun. He kept his rifle on Cade. The mention of my name didn't seem to mean anything to him. If he was our killer, it should have.

"And you," I said, "are Willie Compton. Grandson of Chester Compton. Now that we're acquainted, set the rifle on the floor."

It occurred to me my request might be too much to ask. From the looks of him, it was possible he no longer had the ability to bend over.

"I want my questions answered first."

I reached the bottom of the stairs and stopped. "I'll tell you anything you want to know."

"Why can't I talk to *him*?" he asked, head tipped toward Cade.

"I'm the one with the gun. Why are you here?"

"I saw my grandfather's property on the news. A chopper was filming it from the air. I want to know why."

"You don't know what happened?"

"What do you mean?"

"I take it you didn't watch the entire broadcast?"

He shook his head. "Soon as I saw it, I got in my truck. You gonna tell me what's going on?"

This time he gazed at me just long enough for Cade to lunge forward and battle Willie for the gun. It wasn't much of a fight.

"Don't hurt him," I said.

"Wasn't going to," Cade replied.

Willie's palms went up. "Aww hell."

"I'll answer your questions," I said, "but first I want you to answer some of mine."

"Why would you? I just had a rifle on your...Cade here."

"I don't believe you would have shot him."

"Don't you?" he said. His mouth formed a crooked smile. "Guess you'll never know now. If you're going to ask questions, let's get on with it."

"Did you hire Karin Ackerman to steal from the museum?"

"I might have. What's it matter?"

Blatant honesty was just one of the things I lauded in old-timers. At least he didn't deny it.

"It's important," I said. "I need to know."

"Why? Because the theater blew up and now everyone's curious? What's it got to do with me?"

"Everything."

He crossed his arms. "Oh...I see. You've seen the film, haven't you?"

"You know about the movie?" I asked.

"Melody what's-her-name came to my house, yammered on and on about how she needed my help to get the story right."

"Did you?"

"Slam the door in her face? Sure did."

"What do you know about the explosion?"

"I saw it on television just like everyone else. What are you getting at?"

"You hired someone to steal," I said. "You could have also hired someone to blow up the theater."

He pointed at himself. "You think *I* had something to do with it? So now I'm a killer because my grandfather was one?" His bottom lip trembled. He reached up, attempted to cover it with his hand. "What my grandfather did...to this day, it sickens me."

The emotion seemed genuine. I wanted to believe he was telling the truth.

"If you're innocent, explain what happened at the museum."

"A year ago or so there was a write-up in the paper. A movie was to be made about the murders at the mines. I remember sitting in my recliner thinking it couldn't be true. After all these years, why would anyone want to drudge up the past? Then *she* started calling, and when I refused to talk to her, she came to my house."

"Melody Sinclair obviously valued your input," I said.

"I've lived my entire life harboring regret over what happened to Leonard. For over fifty years, I've relived the same nightmare night after night. You'd think it would go away after a while. It never did."

Losing my own sister had taught me the same thing.

"First to lose a brother," he continued, "then to find out my grandfather, the relative I idolized most, killed seven women then traipsed around like he'd done no wrong. I've had more sleepless nights than all the years of your life. And you think I'd waste the remainder of it killing more innocent people? I don't want to remember my past. I want everyone else to forget it as well."

If Willie was telling the truth, the Compton apple had fallen several acres away from the tree, and Willie wasn't like Chester at all.

"If you didn't bomb the theater, who did? Who else had motive?"

"I don't know."

"I think you do," I said.

"You've been wrong about everything else. Why stop now?"

"You still haven't explained Karin Ackerman."

I felt like a parrot, just press record and pull the string. How many pulls would it take to get an answer?

"Did she tell you I did it?"

"She gave me a physical description," I said. "It's easy to see she was describing you."

"If you think I'm capable of such a thing, why am I still standing here? Take me in, get it over with."

I shot a glance at Cade. "Cuff him."

At present, Cade didn't have any handcuffs in his possession, but Willie only knew Cade was a detective. He didn't know where.

Willie ran two bent, arthritic fingers through his threadlike hair and then tugged the loose skin surrounding his jaw. "Fine, fine. I hired Karin because I knew once the movie came out people would do exactly what you're doing now—go to any length to get more of the story. My family name has been butchered enough. I don't want meddling reporters at my house, ogling the items that tainted our history. I don't want them here, in this house, mixing lies with the truth."

"You just wanted it to go away," I said.

"Can you blame me? How would you feel if it was your family? Your grandfather? Your brother?"

"If you want to get away from the past, why haven't you sold this place?"

He smirked. "I don't want to sell it. I want to burn it to the ground. After all of this happened, after Leonard died and the women were found, the developer who was all set to buy it pulled out. I guess the controversy was too great. Told my dad the thought of buying it after what happened gave him the creeps. Can't say I blamed him. He bought another stretch of property, built a ski resort. My father was so angry he took the house off the market. He was shamed. We all were."

"When the women were discovered in the fifties, you were just a boy," I said. "How much did your parents tell you?"

"As little as possible. Worked for a while. Then one day I was at my aunt's house. I didn't visit very often, and she didn't know it had been kept from me. I learned things I wish I hadn't."

"So you know everything?"

"As much as there is to know."

"Are you married?" I asked. "Do you have any children?"

"No and no. Are you finished?"

I wasn't sure how to broach the subject of what had occurred over the last several days, the last day in particular. "You asked why we're here. I'll tell you. Someone is killing women again, in the same way, and in the same place as before."

Willie staggered back, his face even whiter than before.

"No...no. It's not true. You're lying."

"I would never lie about something like this."

"It can't be. Please...you must be wrong. You must."

CHAPTER 41

It took some time for Willie to settle down once he heard the news. His body seemed to experience the five stages of grief within a matter of minutes. Every second we spent inside Chester's house, I felt colder and colder, and it wasn't just the temperature outside. I didn't want to be here anymore.

"Is there any chance you could help us find the man we're looking for?" I asked.

"How could I? I don't know who he is."

"What about family? Is anyone still alive who might know more?"

He shook his head. "Cousins. They were kids at the time, just like I was. All of my aunts, uncles...they're no longer around."

"Did any of your relatives ever mention anything about your grandfather not working alone?"

"My grandfather's brother speculated as much. No one gave his opinion much consideration though."

"Why?" I asked.

"He refused to believe Chester was guilty, even after all the evidence they found right here in this house."

"Typed pages, a gun, and a piece of fabric, right?"

"They found the typewriter too. Matched it up easily since the letter "e" never showed up right." He closed his eyes. "Miss Monroe. It's not that I don't want to help, but I don't want to know anything more. It's too hard."

"I apologize if we scared you by trespassing," I said. "We just need to find this guy."

"I'm not trying to keep you from doing your job. I hope you find him, for your sake, and for the sake of the women too."

Cade opened the bolt, removing the shell from the rifle's chamber. He handed the gun back to Willie. Willie took it, nodded like he grasped why Cade still felt he needed to err on the side of caution.

On the way out, Willie caught my elbow with his hand. "Walk with me."

I returned him to his truck, noting the identical tires on the front—although I believed he was innocent, I couldn't resist the urge to double check just in case. He pulled on the handle, reached over, lifted a key from an open drawer under the radio. He deposited it in my hand. "18B."

"What's this?"

"A key to a storage unit. Been in my family for years. Before my father died, we came here, packed most of it up. Donated a good portion to charity. A few things my father wanted to keep. I don't know why. Pictures mainly. I didn't want any of it. Still don't. Oh, and...you'll find a grey container. It contains everything I took from the museum. Don't know if it will help, but my conscience won't be clear if it turns out any of it could have made a difference. Do with it what you will."

He slid onto the seat of the truck, started to close the door. I held it open.

"I need to tell you—"

A trio of SUVs, sirens blazing, slid up the drive.

"I'm sorry," I said. "I texted them. I believe you, Willie, I do. But please understand, I need to be a hundred percent sure."

He placed a hand over mine. "It's okay. I've nothing to hide."

"I know it's been a long time, but I want you to know how sorry I am about your brother. I know what it's like to lose a sibling.

"I don't mean to be rude, miss, but not the way he died you don't."

CHAPTER 42

"How long do you think he's had this stuff in storage?" Cade asked.

"No idea."

"Don't they auction a unit off after a certain amount of time?"

"Not as long as you keep paying."

We still had a good amount of daylight left when we located unit 18B at Sunrise Storage. The exterior door was tiny, about four feet wide. Willie was right. They hadn't saved much. The lock was old and weathered, but it still served its purpose just fine. Cade slipped the key into the hole, twisted it to the right. Nothing happened.

"Try wiggling it," I said.

He looked at me like every man does when a woman tries to "help him" do his job. He tried again. His efforts were ineffective.

I placed a hand over his. "Here, let me."

I paused, thinking he'd take even more offense, but he backed away, a look of indifference on his face. Three attempts later and I felt like a failure too.

"I can't believe it," I said.

When Cade didn't reply, I turned to see him back at his truck, milling around in a metal box in the back. He returned, hammer in hand. He pounded the lock and the area surrounding it.

"What are you—"

The lock fell off.

Cade smiled, satisfied with his gallant achievement. "Would you like to do the honors?"

I held my hand out like I was showcasing a prize on a game show. "Go ahead."

The metal door rose. I wasn't sure what I expected to find on the other side—a room stacked full of junky boxes, maybe. It wasn't to be.

"This won't take long," Cade said. "I'm not sure why anyone would keep a storage unit this long with just five boxes in it and some random furniture."

The unit smelled like the final resting place for several generations of rodents. Aside from the boxes there was an antique bike, a dresser, and a desk. The dresser and desk were both empty.

"Why do you think they kept this furniture and got rid of the rest?" Cade asked.

"It looks expensive, or maybe these two items were passed down from a generation or two before."

We opened the boxes, sifted through sterling silverware, heirlooms, albums full of photos. Nothing stood out, not one single thing. In the photos I thumbed through, Chester and Pearl looked like a happy, normal couple.

"I think I see the container Willie mentioned behind this desk," Cade said, strong-arming the desk to the side.

Indeed it was. I set it in front of me, pulled the lid off.

"This is it? I thought there would be more."

Two typed pages, faded so much it was hard to read. None of it made much sense—it was several paragraphs of random, restless babbling. A piece of fabric with flowers on it with an edge that looked like it had been dipped in blood, and newspapers, several of them. There were detailed articles with information about the seven women, the murders, even a graphic sketch someone had drawn recreating the scene at the bottom of the mine. A photo of Chester Compton was front and center on one paper, and a photo of Detective Hurtwick made headline news on the other. The detective posed for the camera in front of the Compton house, typewriter in hand.

I sighed, frustrated. I was no closer to finding the killer than I had been a few hours before. And for Angela Rivers, time was running out.

CHAPTER 43

Carlo was waiting in his car outside when I arrived home. I let him in.

"I wanted to apologize," he said.

Apologies seemed to be running rampant these days.

"Why?"

He glanced at Cade like he was trying to decide whether to continue the conversation in his presence or not. "I...spoke to Giovanni today. I knew you two broke it off, but until today, I didn't know why. He told me."

Nice of Giovanni to keep our private life private. It made me wonder whether Giovanni was keeping in touch with Carlo so he could keep tabs on me. He didn't deserve to know about my life. He no longer had the privilege.

"Why are you sorry?"

"I gave you a hard time. It wasn't your fault."

Cade got up, walked into the other room, giving us our privacy. I didn't want it. Giovanni was a Band-Aid I wasn't ready to rip off yet, let alone discuss at length. I changed the subject. "The gun used to kill the women, if it's the same one as before—"

"I know where you're going with this. And I already checked. Saw it with my own eyes this morning. It's still in evidence. It would have been easy for the Sundance Killer to do his research, find out the type of gun Chester used, buy one similar or the same."

"What about a list of everyone who purchased a forty-five in the area?"

"Like I said, this is what we do," he said. "We haven't made a connection. Believe me, we've tried."

With the conversation going in another direction, Cade returned to the room.

"Your forehead's all wrinkled up," Carlo said to me. "Is something bothering you?"

Cade nodded, agreeing with Carlo's assessment.

"The note the killer left in Shelby's coat, I feel like it was meant for me. I can't help but wonder if I crossed paths with him before. He put himself at risk to give Shelby back, but he did it anyway. It's like he respects me or feels sorry for me, or both."

Carlo crossed one leg over the other. "Maybe you're right and it was for you. What do you think he meant by it?"

I threw my hands in the air. "I don't know."

"Care to find out if you're right?"

"How?"

"I'd like to try out a technique on you," Carlo said. "We use it on witnesses. I've never done it myself, but I've watched it being performed many times."

"Do you mean hypnosis?"

"No. It helps jog the memory. What do you say?"

"Sure, if you think it will work."

"Close your eyes," Carlo said.

"Right now?" I asked.

"Do you have something more important you could be doing?"

He turned toward Cade. "I'll need you to keep quiet."

Cade looked back like he wanted to shove his boot somewhere Carlo wouldn't soon forget.

I leaned back, did what Carlo asked.

"Take yourself back to the beginning when everything first started," he said, "when you returned to Park City the morning after the bombing. Think of all the places you've been, all the people you've seen."

"Okay."

"Now…focus on the people you've come into contact with over the past several days. People you didn't know before."

"It's impossible. I can't register everyone at the same time."

"Your mind can process a lot more than you give it credit for. Relax. Take a deep breath. Try again."

I saw myself in the car with Maddie, at the hospital, the station, home. As Carlo continued talking, images filtered in. Some fuzzy, others clear. I flashed from one person to the next. Random people were everywhere, filling rooms, crowding my brain. Still there was no one of significance. No one who stood out.

"I'm going to give you some key words," Carlo said, "from the scripture found in Shelby's jacket. Listen to them, try to remember if any of the words remind you of a specific time and place. Righteous. Astray. Evil. Fall. Pit. Upright. Good. Possession."

Nothing.

They meant nothing.

I opened my eyes.

"What's wrong?" Carlo asked.

"It's not working. I'm sorry. It's not your fault. I can't seem to focus. I started to, but I don't think this will work on me."

"Do you want to try again?"

"I don't think so."

Carlo patted my leg, stood up. "It will come, and when it does, call me."

...

"How about some wine?" Cade asked.

He found two glasses and poured. I hadn't even said "yes" yet.

I held the glass in front of me. "This might not be the best idea."

"Sure it is. Look at it this way...it's good for your heart. I thought it might help you unwind."

"I had no idea you drank wine."

"I don't," he said, holding it out in front of him, "but this is a lot better than I imagined. I might have to stray from my usual."

Stray.

Something inside my head sparked.

"Don't lead me astray," I said.

He slanted his eyes. "What are you talkin' about, darlin'?"

"Don't lead me astray. I said it to Carlo in the coffee shop the morning after he asked me to help him find Melody."

"I still don't follow."

"There was a guy in there at the time. Plaid Shirt Guy. He had a rough look to him, long beard, hair pulled back into a pony-tail, I think."

"Was he sittin' alone?"

"I was so wrapped up in Carlo, I didn't notice."

"You don't usually miss things."

"I know," I said, "but the conversation with Carlo got heated. I couldn't focus on anything else."

"Why? What was you two talkin' about?"

"I was trying to get Carlo to tell me about Giovanni, to admit Giovanni's role in the family business in exchange for me helping him find Melody Sinclair. At some point, I remember saying to Carlo, 'Don't lead me astray.' I told him I'd take the case, but only if he told me about his family, their business, what they do. Carlo was furious."

"Why?"

"I was talking too loud. Everyone could hear me. Carlo stood up, grabbed my arm, and the guy at the other table got involved. He told Carlo to take his hands off me. Then he asked me if I was okay. The whole thing happened so fast."

"I'm tryin' my best to follow you, I am, but what are you tryin' to tell me?"

"The way I interpret the scripture given to Shelby is this: I was the righteous one, the upright one. Giovanni had confused me with his secrets, caused me to go astray."

"But this man, he couldn't possibly have known Giovanni, right?"

"That's not the point. Let me finish." I was standing now, pacing in front of the sofa. "The man heard our conversation, probably from the beginning. He was sitting there, slurping his coffee, and at some point, he must have felt sorry for me."

"And you think that's why he intervened."

"Yes," I said. "I also think he felt I was owed something. The end of that verse says the upright, meaning me, would have good things in my possession."

Cade smacked his hands together. "Shelby."

"I'd been done a wrong, and he made it right. He gave her back."

"It's crazy."

"Not really," I said. "Not to him. This guy sees himself as someone who has been granted a higher power to see justice is carried out, both good and bad. I'd be willing to bet he's rescued a cat and killed someone all in the same day, and he probably didn't think twice about it."

"You have no idea who he is though."

"Yes, I believe I do," I said. "I may not have noticed everything, but I noticed one thing—when he asked me if I was all right, I looked right at him, into his dark, beady eyes. Eyes that looked too small for his face."

I'd seen those eyes before.

CHAPTER 44

I called Carlo, explained my theory. The man at the café had the same eyes as the man in the photo I'd seen earlier of Detective Hurtwick. Butch thought Chester had a partner. But I bet he never would have believed it could have been the good detective.

Carlo was on his way back to Giovanni's estate in Salt Lake City. He flipped around, said he'd drop by the Hurtwick residence, see if my theory amounted to anything before taking further action. He wanted me to sit home, wait for his call.

Not a chance.

I let him know I'd meet him there. Cade grabbed his coat just as Maddie arrived with Shelby. I tried convincing Cade to stay. I'd meet up with Carlo, I'd be all right. But he was just as stubborn as I was, and Shelby relished the opportunity to spend more time with Maddie. I couldn't say I blamed her.

• • •

The Hurtwick residence was at the end of a long, quiet road. A snippet of light shone through the closed shades on the other side of the window pane in the front window. I hoped this meant someone was still awake.

Carlo opened the passenger-side door. I stepped onto sheets of hardened ice.

"I'd like Cade to stay in the car," Carlo said. "It's bad enough you're here. If this turns out to be the lead we're looking for, let me take over."

I resisted the urge to slap him. "Gee, thanks."

Carlo turned. "You misunderstand me."

"I'm guessing you've been told to stay away from me, keep me off the case. I don't have a shiny badge like you do. I get it."

"You're brilliant, Sloane. The way your mind works sometimes is…fascinating. Why do you think I spent time trying to get into it tonight? All I meant to say was—"

"I'm freezing. Can we get this over with?"

While Cade kept the car warm, I tapped on the door. A faint, "Hold on just a minute," echoed from inside. The voice was soft and light, a woman's. The porch light flipped on. Two cats sprung free when the door opened, bounding into the darkness.

"Toodles! Mitsy!" the woman shouted. "Get back here!"

The felines didn't give her a second glance.

"Oh no," she sighed. "It's dark out. Once they're out of the yard, I'll never find them."

"I'll grab them for you," Carlo said, clicking on a high-powered flashlight.

While Carlo commenced Operation Kitty Roundup, I charmed an exhausted looking, fussy, Mrs. Hurtwick, and gained entrance inside. I explained who we were and promised we wouldn't stay long. She shuffled me into the living room, fidgeted with the sleeve of her nightgown until Carlo returned, one fur ball clutched in each hand.

"Whatever you're here for, why can't it wait until morning?" she asked.

"We're looking for a missing girl," I said. "We were hoping to speak to your husband, Detective Hurtwick."

"Arthur? He lives with the Lord now."

One of her eyes was half open, the other almost shut. I wasn't sure we'd be able to keep her awake long enough to get any good information.

Carlo took the lead. "Do you have any children?"

"A son, why?"

"Where is he living?" he asked.

She pointed toward the ceiling.

Dead as well. Terrific.

"I'd like to know how he died."

"I'm not comfortable talking about it."

She was testing the wrong person.

"I need you to answer the question," Carlo prompted. "Right now."

She grabbed a half-finished scarf she'd been knitting, went to work on it. "My son shot himself in his garage."

"How long ago?"

"Two years."

"Why did he take his own life?"

"Forgive me, I fail to see where this conversation is going. There are other ways to get answers to your questions. Do your research, for heaven's sake."

He was losing her.

I looked around, spying several pictures on the mantle over the fireplace. I walked over, picked one up. "Who's this?"

"My son," she replied. "Now please put it down."

I looked at Cade. "Too old."

Similar face though, same eyes.

"Did your son have any children?" Carlo asked.

"Two, yes. One boy, one girl."

"Can I see a recent photo of your grandchildren?"

"I want you to leave. I'm tired."

Carlo took the knitting from her hands, set it down. "I can take you in if you choose not to cooperate."

"You can't just haul me down there because you feel like it. I invited you into my home, without asking to see a warrant, I might add."

"This isn't the fifties, Mrs. Hurtwick. And I'm FBI, not a detective like your late husband." He pulled a photo out of his pocket, shoved it right in her face. "This is Angela Rivers. She's missing. By tomorrow she'll be dead, if she isn't already."

"Why are you telling *me*? I can't help you."

"You can," he said.

"Why are you asking about my family?"

Paranoia set in. Carlo zeroed in on it and mellowed. He sat beside her, smiled, gave an impression like everything was fine. "We have reason to believe your grandson knows the person who took our missing girl."

The lie worked. Her body relaxed, her eyes softened.

"You mean to say Shawn witnessed it—he was there at the time?"

Shawn Hurtwick.

We had a name.

I texted Cade, asked him to search for a Shawn Hurtwick in the area.

"Shawn might have seen something, yes," Carlo responded.

She looked scared. "I don't know. He asked me not to say anything to anyone. He said some bad people might come around asking questions. He said not to answer them or his life would be in danger."

"When was this?"

"Two weeks ago, when he came back."

"Came back from where?" Carlo asked.

"After his father died he left, quit his job, said he wanted to see the world. I think traveling was a way for him to deal with the grief."

Or a way to lurk around the set of a movie.

"Where did your son work?"

"He was a contractor. He was always good at building things, making things, ever since he was a boy."

"When he left, did he fly or drive?" Carlo asked.

"He left his daddy's Ford here. Wouldn't have lasted one day on a road trip."

A Ford which I was willing to bet had two different front tires.

"Do you know where your grandson is right now?"

"I can't," she responded. "I promised."

Carlo switched again. He spewed threats, frightening her.

There were two halls in Mrs. Hurtwick's house. I picked one when she wasn't looking, found the master bedroom at the end of the hall. There had to be a photo of Shawn Hurtwick somewhere.

A return text came in from Cade. There was no address for a Shawn Hurtwick. He'd owned a home in Park City, but sold it a couple years earlier. There was, however, an address for Roy, Shawn's deceased father.

A tray rested on top of a long dresser. On it were two bottles of the same perfume. Lavender Nostalgia.

Lavender.

I tore down the hall, yelling. "Carlo—"

A gunshot went off.

Mrs. Hurtwick screamed.

CHAPTER 45

Shawn Hurtwick stood over Carlo, a .45 Colt in his hand. Blood oozed from the back of Carlo's head, spilling onto the rug below. He wasn't moving. I'd picked the wrong hallway. Shawn must have been hiding, listening the entire time.

Outside, footsteps approached.

Cade.

Shawn steadied the gun, zeroed in on the front door.

Too late.

I fired.

Shawn turned, disillusioned. He didn't think I would shoot him. The bullet cut through his shoulder, exactly where I wanted it to go. Dying was too easy. His victims deserved more.

"This him?" Cade asked. "This the guy who took my daughter?"

I nodded.

Cade balled his fist, drilled it into the side of Shawn's head. Shawn went down. Cade swung his boot backward and launched it forward, over and over again into Shawn's chest. Shawn cried out. Mrs. Hurtwick screamed again, but she knew better than to move.

I collapsed to the floor next to Carlo, frantically pressing numbers on my phone. I held the phone to my ear, waiting for it to ring. It didn't. Water filled my eyes. "Hang on, Carlo, hang on!" I wanted to beat my phone against the wall. "Why isn't this working?!"

"Sloane…"

Cade stood over me, hand out.

My voice was shaky, trembling. "I don't know why it's not working. I can't get it to work, Cade."

"Let me do it. I'll make the call."

"We need an ambulance…and I need…I need…the chief."

"I know. I'll take care of it."

His voice was soft, reassuring, but it didn't quell the pain inside. Cade dialed with one hand, kept his gun directed at Shawn with the other, even though he wasn't moving. Mrs. Hurtwick tried to rise. Cade stopped her.

"Sit," he warned.

"Carlo…can you hear me?" I straddled Carlo's body, felt for a pulse. There wasn't one. Cade bent down, looked him over, sheathed an arm around me.

"There's nothin' you can do for him now, darlin'."

It couldn't be. This wasn't happening.

I broke free from Cade's grip, cradled Carlo in my arms, his blood soaking my shirt.

Shawn groaned as he flipped around, his gaze fixed on me.

"Why?" I asked. "Why did you have to take his life?"

"To deliver thee from the way of the evil *man*."

Cade stared at Shawn, stunned.

"Stop it! Just stop," I said. "No more."

Shawn's face twisted into a wicked smiled. "But you said you understand."

"I don't. I never will."

"He had to die. He was going to hurt my nana. I popped him before he even knew I was there."

Shawn laughed. I eased Carlo back down, lunged, slapped Shawn in the face.

"Where's Angela Rivers?!" I yelled.

He didn't answer.

"I will *find* her."

"I'm sure you will."

"Your grandfather, he was in it together with Chester Compton, wasn't he?"

"Still so wrong, Miss Monroe. How does it feel?"

"How does *what* feel?"

"Failure."

"Enough," Cade ordered, "or I'll shoot you myself."

"Shawn, what is she talking about?" Mrs. Hurtwick asked. "What did your grandfather do?"

"Not now, Nana," Shawn replied.

"She deserves to know the truth," I said. "And you should be the one to tell it to her."

"I won't."

"Yes, you will, Shawn," Mrs. Hurtwick said. "Look at me."

He stared up at her.

"If there's something I need to know, you tell me right now," she said.

Shawn wasn't talking.

"Do you remember the seven women who were found murdered in the fifties, the ones Chester Compton killed?" I asked.

"Of course I do," she said. "My Arthur proved Chester Compton was guilty. Chester was a horrible, evil man."

"No, Nana," Shawn said. "He wasn't."

"What do you mean, Shawn? Of course he was."

"Chester Compton never murdered those women. Grandpa did."

Detective Hurtwick had covered it up, planted the evidence in Chester Compton's house. I'd been so wrong.

"Who helped him?" I asked. "He didn't do it alone."

"My dad."

Mrs. Hurtwick was wailing now, finally realizing the gravity of the situation.

"But your father would have only been—"

"A teenager at the time, yes."

"Do you see now? Do you see why I had to crush the lie?"

"You didn't have to kill innocent people to prove your point," I said.

"They deserved to die."

The front door blew open.

Armed men charged forward.

It was all over.

CHAPTER 46

Angela Rivers was found in the basement of Roy Hurtwick's home, alive, strapped to a chair with duct tape, but otherwise unharmed. The only reason she'd survived was because Shawn was creating a new burial chamber for the three remaining women he never had the chance to take, and it wasn't finished yet.

When questioned, Shawn spilled it all, proclaiming his actions were justified. He said it all began when his father confessed the truth about Shawn's grandfather—the night before his father took his own life. Apparently Roy had stopped by Shawn's home, desperate and forlorn because he'd just walked in on his wife, Shawn's stepmother, catching her in bed with another man.

"Your grandfather was right," he'd said to Shawn. "The evil ones need to be punished."

In his hands, Roy carried a white, cardboard box. "Come here, I want to show you something," Roy had said.

They sat down together. Roy told Shawn about the murders, explained how Shawn's grandfather, Detective Hurtwick, falsely accused Chester Compton. "It was easy. Your grandfather was a detective, well respected. No one questioned his judgment, and no one had any reason to believe Chester Compton wasn't guilty."

Roy lifted the lid, removed a gun, a Colt .45. He said they'd purchased a pair of them together. One was planted at the fake crime scene; the other was saved as a memento. Detective Hurtwick hoped one day it would be passed down. At the prompting of his father, Roy tried killing once, but he botched the job. He'd shot the woman, but she hadn't died, so he had to fire two more times. Then he vomited and had to call his father for help. In Roy's opinion, Detective Arthur Hurtwick was a saint, but Roy couldn't bring himself to do what his dad had done.

For years before his confession Shawn had felt urges, an overwhelming desire to kill, but he fought it, never understanding why he wasn't like everyone else. When he looked at the box in his father's hands that night, felt the weight of the pistol, ran his fingers over the pieces of cut fabric taken from each woman's clothing as a souvenir, he had been conflicted.

A fire was burning hard and strong inside him, a yearning.

The last thing Roy had said to his son that night was, "It's up to us to make them pay."

The next day Roy took his own life, but not before posting a letter to Shawn in the mail. In the letter he admitted to ending his own life because he couldn't bring himself to kill his wife, even after what she'd done. Roy felt like he had failed his father for so long, saying even though his dad was dead, he could feel his father's presence, watching, waiting. Roy couldn't live any longer, knowing he'd been such a disappointment.

Upon reading the letter, Shawn had been enraged.

And then the trigger came. The event he needed to satisfy his desires. The local news interviewed a woman making a movie about a dark time in Park City's history. She'd named it *Bed of Bones*. He stared at the screen, watching her talk about Chester Compton, about the murders, facilitating lies for the world to see. It was time people learned the truth. They deserved the truth. He would find the woman, set her straight.

He'd set them all straight.

CHAPTER 47

Records from the original investigation proved Hurtwick was the one who'd verified Chester Compton purchased the Colt pistol. Since the gun shop was still around, Chief Sheppard ordered a subsequent visit. Hurtwick had lied, just like he'd lied about everything.

Shawn was alive and awaiting a court date. It was no surprise the state was going for the death penalty. I saw death by way of lethal injection in his future.

I gave Willie the good news about his grandfather in person. When I finished, I handed him the box of photos from the storage unit, figuring he'd want them now. He broke down, shedding tears of joy. His only wished his father would have lived long enough to know the truth. I only wished Carlo could have shared the moment with me.

Carlo's ceremony was held in New York City. I wasn't invited, and I didn't care. I attended anyway, strolled right up to the third pew and sat down. Daniela recognized me first. She whispered in Giovanni's ear. His eye bulged when he saw me. He said something to an olive-skinned brunette to his left. She was clutching his arm with her hand like she was drowning and he was her life preserver. He started to stand.

I shook my head, crossed my arms.

Not today, you don't.

I didn't want him to get the wrong idea. I was there for Carlo, whom, after the recent time we'd spent together, I had come to know in a different way. It saddened me to witness Giovanni's grief first-hand, but I couldn't talk to him, not yet. It didn't matter how many times Chief Sheppard reminded me of Angela Rivers and the other potential lives I'd saved, I couldn't get away from the lives I'd lost.

The olive-skinned brunette girl glanced back at me, flicked her hair, scowled, a look most unbecoming of a lady. If we hadn't been in a church I might have returned the gesture with one of my own. Instead, I met her gaze, smiled. She could have him—the secrets, the lies, all of it.

An older man sitting on the other side of Daniela said something to her then made the slightest movement with his head. He didn't want me to catch him looking, even though I had anyway. I was two for two in the icy-glare department.

The services came to an end and I slipped out, hailing the cab I'd paid to wait for me. An exasperated Giovanni sprung from the cathedral doors just in time to see the cab whiz down the road. He was too late.

CHAPTER 48

One month later Maddie extended an invitation to Shelby to attend a seminar she was hosting at a convention center in Salt Lake City on the dissection of human cadavers. Maddie was certain Shelby had a promising future in the forensics department. Shelby agreed.

After the conference Cade and Shelby stuck around for the weekend. Although Cade hadn't said it out loud, he was worried about me. I could tell. Over the last month I hadn't taken on any new cases and I hadn't returned any work-related calls. I hadn't done much of anything. Cade practically dragged me, but he managed to get me out of the house.

The sedan tailing us from behind was a plain, blend-in-with-the-snow shade of white. This could have been the reason why it took me so long to recognize we were being followed. I firmly believed over half of all Utahns drove white cars. In Utah, a white paint job and a multi-passenger minivan was as abundant as an orange grove in Florida.

"I'm in desperate need of a chai tea. Can we stop?" I reached into my purse, pulled out my wallet, handed Shelby a hundred-dollar bill. Cade tried to object. I cut him off.

"This shop has the best clothes in town," I said to Shelby. "Go in, see what you think. And take your time. We're not in a hurry."

She waved the crisp bill in front of her dad's face, her eyes dancing with excitement. Who knew it was this easy to satisfy a teenager?

"Thanks!" She looked at Cade. "Dad, can we keep her?"

He laughed. "We'll see."

I turned to Cade. "I'll get out here as well."

"No, you won't. The coffee shop is on the other end. I'll drive you. We'll grab the tea you can't live without, swing back here, and wait for Shelby."

I was hoping by this time Shelby would have high-tailed it into the dress shop. She waited.

I held a finger up, silencing Cade.

"I'll walk. I need the fresh air. You stay here."

The only fresh air I willingly participated in was the kind that accompanied spring or summer. But I saw no other way. Cade eyed me through the rear-view

mirror like I was deranged. I dipped into the dressing
room of the dress shop, hung up the decoy skirt I never
intended to try on, and sent Cade a text. Then I embraced
the cold again, peering through shop windows along the
way like I was trying to decide whether or not I wanted
to go inside.

The frigid air nipped at my fingers, numbed my
toes. I shoved my ungloved hands inside my coat pocket,
swished them around, tried to generate even the smallest
amount of heat. Not much longer and I'd reach the finish
line where a white sedan was waiting, its motor
humming, low and still.

I didn't glance at the car when I crossed the street,
passing in front of it. I entered the coffee shop, ordered,
and slid into a booth. I sipped my tea, breathed, counted
the sugar packets inside a rectangular bowl in front of
me. Waited.

A man wielding a wooden cane sat across from me
in the booth. He slung the side of the cane over one knee
exposing the top, arched silver shaped like the head of a
serpent. The eyes were red. Rubies. I stared at the gems,
he stared at me.

"Can I help—"

Before I'd uttered the "you," part of the sentence, I'd
bravely taken a closer look at his face. His jawline was
square and defined, like Giovanni's. His fingers strong

and wide, like Carlo's. And even though I'd only seen the side of his face at the funeral, he wasn't hard to identify.

"Sloane Monroe," he said, his voice intrepid, unwavering. "I've heard a great deal about you."

"Why are you here? Do you blame me for what happened to Carlo? You got Giovanni back. Isn't that what you wanted?"

He twisted his lips into something resembling a smile, but it was like he'd forgotten how to show true sincerity. "I need to be sure you won't come after him. I've lost one son to you, I won't lose the other."

It wasn't in me to chase after any man, but I wasn't about to give him the satisfaction.

"What I do or don't do isn't any of your business."

He leaned forward. "My dear, *everything* is my business."

I fingered my gun under the table. "I'm not your *dear.*"

He laughed. "Fiesty little thing, aren't you?"

"Get up and get out," I said. "I'll only say it once."

I wondered if any woman had ever spoken to him like this before. I felt honored if I was the first. He was old. I didn't care who he was or what he was. All I saw was a fragile, worn-out bully who belonged in a rest home, not sitting in front of me, in my town, in my territory.

"We will sit here as long as it takes for you to listen," he said.

"I believe I made myself clear. And now I'm getting up, and you're leaving town."

He turned his palms up. "The choice is yours. I will have my say, one way or the other. If necessary, you can join me, and we'll take a ride." He paused then said, "I can understand now what my son sees in you, what they all see in you, but don't misunderstand the affection I have for my children to mean I'd hesitate to spare your life."

He said this thinking it would create a sense of shock and awe. I stood. "Fine. You stay I'll leave."

"Do you think I go anywhere unprepared?" he quipped. "I've been at this a lot longer than you, my dear. You have a single gun. Your hand is probably resting on the hardened steel right now, feeling it, trying to decide what you want to do. Look behind me. See the white car in the parking lot? Good. Now look inside."

"Oh, I'm looking. I'm just not seeing."

"Look again," he said, without turning around. "Pay particular attention to the two gunmen sitting in the front seat. They're my men, you see. Two men, two guns. Drawn, I might add. All they need is for me to raise two fingers. So you see, I have two guns pointed at you right now."

"Had," Cade said, coming up from behind. "Anticipation is everything."

Mr. Luciana turned, staring unaffected into Cade's eyes. Outside his so-called gunmen were being escorted into the back of one of Chief Sheppard's squad cars, their pistols, confiscated. This time when Mr. Luciana smiled, it was as genuine as the rubies staring through the eyes of the snake. He saw Chief Sheppard. He saw Coop. He didn't know who they were, but he didn't have to—he was familiar with the drill.

"I have to admit," he said, gazing at the two of us, "this is a shock. And what a pleasant one."

At first I didn't grasp his meaning. He looked at Cade, who was looking at me, and he was pleased. "Maybe my coming here wasn't necessary after all."

Mr. Luciana tried placing a hand inside his breast pocket. Cade stopped him. "Relax," he said. "I'm just getting my cell phone."

Cade reached out, snatched it away from him. "Not today, you're not."

CHAPTER 49

I leaned over the sink in my bathroom, gazed into the mirror, for the first time realizing it wasn't just me I saw staring back. It was my sister. Ever since her death, I'd kept my hair long. I hadn't changed the color. I hadn't changed the style.

Maybe because it reminded me of her.

Or maybe because it made me feel like she was still with me.

I wasn't sure why I hadn't noticed it before. It was just one more thing holding me back, keeping me from embracing my own future. For all of the advice I'd given Shelby about moving on with her life, suddenly I felt like a hypocrite.

I pulled open the top drawer, took out a pair of scissors, sliced them together in the air. Still sharp. I held them up to my ears and cut.

Things were about to change.

THE END

All of Cheryl Bradshaw's novels are heavily researched, proofed, edited, and professionally formatted by a skilled team of professionals. Should you find any errors, please contact the author directly. Her assistant will forward the issue(s) to the publisher. It's our goal to present you with the best possible reading experience, and we appreciate your help in making that happen. You can contact the author through her website cherylbradshaw.com.

About Cheryl Bradshaw

Cheryl Bradshaw is a *USA Today* bestselling author. She currently has two series: Sloane Monroe mystery/thriller series and the Addison Lockhart paranormal suspense series. Stranger in Town (Sloane Monroe series #4) was a 2013 Shamus Award finalist for Best PI Novel of the Year, and I Have a Secret (Sloane Monroe series #3) was a 2013 eFestival of Words winner for best thriller novel. To learn more:

Website: cherylbradshaw.com
Facebook: Cheryl Bradshaw Books
Twitter: @cherylbradshaw
Blog: cherylbradshawbooks.blogspot.com

And sign up for my quarterly author newsletter on my blog.

Enjoy the Story?

If you enjoyed *Bed of Bones*, you can show your appreciation by leaving a review on Amazon, Barnes & Noble, iTunes, or in the Sony Kobo Store. I'm always grateful when a reader takes time out of their day to comment on my novels.

If you do write a review, please be sure to email me at cherylbradshawbooks@yahoo.com so I can express my gratitude.

Also by Cheryl Bradshaw

Sloane Monroe Series

Black Diamond Death

Sinnerman

I Have a Secret

Stranger in Town

Bed of Bones

Addison Lockhart Series

Grayson Manor Haunting

Till Death do us Part Short Story Series

Whispers of Murder

Echoes of Murder

Boxed Sets

Sloane Monroe Series (Books 1-3)

Made in the USA
Monee, IL
28 January 2020